There was a bang.

Loud enough to get his attention above the raging water. Someone in the trunk screamed for help. Charlotte was still alive.

"I'm coming! Hang on!" He grabbed the latch on the back.

"Hurry, we don't have much time," she called.

We? She wasn't alone. Jonas struggled with the handle while watching the rising water claim more of the sinking vehicle.

When the door finally released, the deputy's huge green eyes met Jonas's. "Help me get her out before it goes under. She's been shot."

"I've got her." But getting the injured woman from the Jeep wasn't easy. The fear in the young woman's eyes urged him on.

"The Jeep is going to take us down with it," Charlotte said. "We've got to get away."

"*Jah*...yes," he corrected quickly. Even though he wasn't Amish anymore, Jonas had gotten accustomed to using Pennsylvania Dutch in his thoughts. Letting go of the old ways was hard.

"Let's try to make it to the bank." Charlotte swam out in front of him. From where he was now, the riverbank appeared miles away.

Mary Alford was inspired to become a writer after reading romantic suspense greats Victoria Holt and Phyllis A. Whitney. Soon, creating characters and throwing them into dangerous situations that tested their faith came naturally for Mary. In 2012, Mary entered the speed dating contest hosted by Love Inspired Suspense and later received "the call." Writing for Love Inspired Suspense has been a dream come true for Mary.

Books by Mary Alford

Love Inspired Suspense

Forgotten Past
Rocky Mountain Pursuit
Deadly Memories
Framed for Murder
Standoff at Midnight Mountain
Grave Peril
Amish Country Kidnapping
Amish Country Murder
Covert Amish Christmas
Shielding the Amish Witness
Dangerous Amish Showdown
Snowbound Amish Survival
Amish Wilderness Survival
Amish Country Ransom
Deadly Mountain Escape

Visit the Author Profile page at LoveInspired.com.

DEADLY MOUNTAIN ESCAPE

MARY ALFORD

LOVE INSPIRED SUSPENSE
INSPIRATIONAL ROMANCE

LOVE INSPIRED® SUSPENSE
INSPIRATIONAL ROMANCE

ISBN-13: 978-1-335-59932-2

Deadly Mountain Escape

Recycling programs for this product may not exist in your area.

For questions and comments about the quality of this book, please contact us at CustomerService@Harlequin.com.

Love Inspired
22 Adelaide St. West, 41st Floor
Toronto, Ontario M5H 4E3, Canada
www.LoveInspired.com

Printed in U.S.A.

And God shall wipe away all tears from their eyes;
and there shall be no more death, neither sorrow,
nor crying, neither shall there be any more pain:
for the former things are passed away.

—Revelation 21:4

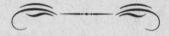

To my mom and dad.
Thank you for starting me on this amazing journey.

ONE

Deputy Charlotte Walker stepped out onto the porch. Her neighbor Dottie Marques turned troubled eyes her way. "I know it's hard, but please try not to worry," Charlotte said. "I'm sure there's a valid explanation for why she didn't come home after work last night." Yet the pit in Charlotte's stomach disagreed with those words.

"Thank you," Dottie said. "I know I'm probably being an overprotective grandmother, but Lainey is the only family I have, and she wouldn't stay away so long without calling." The older woman shuddered. "I'm so afraid. I can't lose her."

"This will help." Charlotte held up the pink argyle garment that belonged to Lainey. "Annie should be able to get Lainey's scent from it."

Dottie's eyes were red and swollen from crying. "You'll call as soon as you know anything?"

Charlotte nodded. "I'll start at the Christian youth camp you said Lainey likes to visit. She may very well be there and can't get service enough to check in with you. That part of the county is remote."

Dottie clutched Charlotte's hands. "From your lips to God's ears."

Charlotte's family and the Marques family had owned neighboring ranches in the Ruby Valley of Montana for several generations. After Dottie's husband died, she'd managed the ranch on her own until Lainey came to live with her a few years back. When Charlotte's parents both died soon after each other, she wouldn't have gotten through without Dottie. The woman was forged in steel and Montana strong.

"Stay close to the phone in case Lainey calls. If you do hear from her, let me know."

"Find her, Charlotte. Please."

"I will. I promise." With a heartbreaking plea from a desperate grandmother still ringing in her ears, Charlotte prayed she'd be able to back it up. "Stay strong. For Lainey."

When Dottie called for help, Charlotte couldn't refuse. So, off duty and out of uniform, she headed for her bright yellow Jeep parked in the drive. Annie, her K-9 partner, waited in the passenger seat, eyes glued to Charlotte.

Annie was a bluetick coonhound with a unique tricolored coat that was predominately dark blue in color. She had black spots on her back, ears and sides known as ticking. Charlotte placed Lainey's sweater on the center console and waved to Dottie as she drove away.

Annie sniffed the sweater as if sensing her skills were about to be put to the test.

"Are you ready to get to work? Dottie needs our help." Annie's enthusiastic woof had Charlotte smiling despite her pressing concern for Lainey's safety. Lainey might be twenty and an adult, but she would never do anything to cause her grandmother undue worry. Disappearing for any length of time without calling wasn't like her.

Charlotte drove toward the deserted place in the wilderness where the Christian camp was located, not far from the Tobacco Root Mountains. Memories of the last missing person case she'd worked on in that area came to mind. Michaela Reagan's case had cost Charlotte personally. She'd lost her fiancé, Ryan—a K-9 trainer and member of the county's search and rescue team—when Ryan fell to his death while assisting with Michaela's search.

Law enforcement, along with the county's SAR team, had searched tirelessly throughout the night only to find the missing teen dead at the base of Hollowtop Mountain. She'd been shot once in the head. The gun was found lying near her body. The cause of death was ruled suicide, yet many believed the scene was staged.

Charlotte was among them. Michaela was a well-liked teen from a prominent and loving family. Why would she shoot herself? Could her death have anything to do with the mysterious call Charlotte had gotten a week before?

Something deep inside her itched for more answers about her fiancé's death, too. But she never allowed herself to think on it too long. Too painful.

She would never forget Ryan's funeral. Even after hearing Ryan's best friend, Phillip, give the eulogy—watching as the dirt was placed over Ryan's coffin at the graveyard—Charlotte still hadn't been able to grasp the reality that he was really gone until much later.

Charlotte glanced briefly at her partner. Annie was the last dog Ryan had ever trained and more than a friend for Charlotte. She and Annie had continued to grieve Ryan's death throughout this past year he'd been gone. The winter months had been the hardest. She had too much time on her hands. Work helped. Still, each day came with its own pain. Every step forward hurt; Ryan still claimed her heart.

Charlotte turned onto the small dirt road that headed toward the Christian camp. After the camp's closure several years back, the woods had slowly been reclaiming the small lane used to access the site. Lainey would have had to park on the side of this road and hike in.

A strange place for a young woman to go alone, yet Dottie had told her that Lainey went there to get closer to God.

As Charlotte passed the first house down the road, she spotted a man she'd met on a couple different occasions repairing his fence. Jonas Knowles's dark blond hair was covered by a straw hat that looked as if it had seen better days. He wore a dark blue shirt, jeans and suspenders. She remembered Jonas in particular because he had the most unusual shade of blue eyes. Ice blue. The kind you didn't forget.

She waved. Jonas removed his hat and scraped back his hair before returning her greeting.

Living in the shadow of the Tobacco Root Mountains, her family's ranch in the Ruby Valley had been Charlotte's home all her life. She was familiar with just about everyone in the county where she served as a deputy. Her parents had raised her to have faith and be strong. Her dad had been sheriff here for almost five years before he'd retired to care for his ailing wife. Dad had survived countless attacks from both knives and guns, but losing his wife of forty years was something he couldn't overcome. He'd died a few months after his wife.

Even though almost five years had passed, the

pain of their deaths was always close, yet something her father told her shortly before his death came to mind. He'd told her focusing on the past was the surest way to stop moving forward. She'd tried to abide by those words, but this past year had been hard.

As she neared the place where the former camp road had been, an uneasy feeling grasped Charlotte and wouldn't let go. Past Jonas Knowles's place, the trees appeared to grow closer to the road, giving the area a sinister look. The perfect place to cover up a crime if one was looking to do so. Madison County had its share of unsavory suspects who would do whatever was necessary to stay out of prison.

The Christian campsite was a few miles in and on privately owned land. The rest of the property on the right of the road was all national forest. Following an instinct Charlotte couldn't explain, she pulled over onto the edge of the road and grabbed her Kevlar vest from the back seat. Once it was secured in place, she held the sweater out for Annie to get a scent.

As soon as she opened the Jeep's door, Charlotte noticed a set of tire tracks near where she'd parked. Someone had been here at one time. Before she could investigate, Annie bounded from the vehicle. After a few sniffs on the ground, she had her scent and was running with it.

Charlotte scrambled after her partner. Annie moved quickly when on a scent. There was no time to hesitate if Charlotte wanted to keep up with the dog.

Her bright orange K-9 vest made her easy to spot most times, except when traveling through thick brush like now—most of it was taller than the dog.

It took a moment to home in on Annie's direction through the undergrowth. She was heading away from the campsite. Why would Lainey have gone this way?

Charlotte picked up the trail and raced after her partner while her fear for Lainey's safety grew. Even if Lainey had intended to spend some time at the camp, she recognized the area well enough not to get this far off trail.

Yet Lainey had definitely been down this way at some point recently, either by her own volition or by someone else's. Charlotte's shoulders grew tense at the thought of her friend being taken against her will.

Once more she lost track of Annie in the thigh-deep brush. Charlotte stopped and spun around while a sliver of fear wound itself tight in her head. She'd come here alone with only her K-9 partner. Charlotte should have called someone to let them know her location. Dottie knew about the Christian campsite, but as she recalled, there was more than one way to reach it, so it might take searchers longer to find her.

She pulled her phone from her jeans pocket and checked. The no service indicator mocked her mistake. As a deputy for the Madison County Sheriff's Department, the right thing to do was to backtrack until she was able to call her dispatcher and apprise her of what was happening just in case.

But Annie was on track…

Charlotte picked up the dog's location once more and made the decision to keep going. As she walked, she shoved back brush that made moving through it nearly impossible.

After several miles of fast-paced moving, she noticed the woods ahead had been cleared away around a rundown piece of property. It took Charlotte a second to gain her bearings but when she did, she realized she knew the house and its owner quite well. A man by the name of Harley Owens had been in and out of jail for abusing his wife since Charlotte had joined the force.

On multiple occasions Charlotte been called out here on domestic abuse reports…and then his wife would refuse to press charges, claim to have fallen down the steps or something similar.

Tension coiled down deep in her body. Charlotte immediately unholstered her weapon. Harley was dangerous and had gone on record many times bragging about the number of weapons he owned. He'd managed to beat all charges brought against him. Partly because his wife refused to testify, but mostly because Phillip Hollins, the county's district attorney, had said they didn't have enough evidence to convict Harley.

If Lainey's trail led here, there was reason to be concerned.

She approached the dilapidated, peeling white house with caution. Annie had disappeared around the corner of the structure.

An out of place noise coming from the direction Annie had disappeared had Charlotte slowly advancing. She flattened herself against the wall of the house and peeked around, her heart in her throat. Where was Harley? She hadn't seen his beat-up pickup truck parked in the front yard like normal. She listened carefully. No sound came from inside the house. Harley's wife, Betty, didn't work to Charlotte's knowledge. Where was she?

Charlotte dialed 9-1. Before she hit the last 1, a sound almost too faint to hear had her whipping around. She caught sight of a man in a mask before something was shoved against her side. A sharp electrical current sent her to her knees. She'd been Tased. Her attacker snatched her weapon and phone away from her unresisting hands. Another fierce blast from the Taser proved this was deadly serious. She had to get away if she stood a chance at surviving. Charlotte began crawling away from her attacker, but she was weak and barely able to move. She was now in a fight for her life to survive a man who clearly had everything to lose.

Jonas Knowles wiped his forehead as he surveyed the fence line. As much as he wanted to get it finished today, the woman he'd recognized as a deputy for the county wouldn't get out of his head. It had been several hours since she'd passed his place. The only other residence down the dead-end road was Harley's. She hadn't been going there on official business because she was in her personal vehicle. Why had she come down this way in the first place?

He'd spotted the dog with her. Jonas recalled she was part of the sheriff's K-9 unit.

It didn't matter what her business was; it didn't concern him. He jabbed the post hole digger into the earth as her name teased around the edges of his memory. Walker. Charlotte Walker. She'd stopped by to ask Jonas questions about Harley the couple of times she'd been out here. She'd seemed nice enough. Efficient. Though she was petite, he had no doubt she could handle herself. Her sharp green eyes seemed to key in on him. He had no doubt she'd seen the guilt Jonas harbored in his heart.

After he finished the post he'd been working on, Jonas stabbed the post hole digger into the next spot and then headed up to his house for a drink.

Though it was technically springtime in the shadow of the Root Mountains, today had been a hot one.

Jonas reached the porch and opened the screen door. He let it slam behind him. In the kitchen, he poured cold water from the pitcher chilling in the battery-powered fridge and stared out the window toward Harley's place.

In the six years he'd lived here, Jonas had seen things that didn't sit right with him. More than once, he'd come to the defense of Harley's wife, Betty, after he'd heard screaming coming from their house. He'd tried to get Betty to leave her abusive husband, but she was more afraid of what Harley would do to her if she did leave than if she stayed. Harley never seemed to end up in jail for long. And there were all sorts of strange comings and goings at the place all hours of the night.

For someone who had lived twenty-six years of his life as Amish, the activity coming from Harley's was troubling. More than once, Jonas had debated selling his home, even if it meant taking a loss, and finding another piece of property as far away from Harley as possible.

Each time he considered it, he remembered

Betty and realized he couldn't abandon her to Harley's violence. Even if she wouldn't accept his help, he'd be there for her. When she fled her house to get away from her husband, Jonas offered her a safe place to stay and volunteered to ride to the nearest neighbor and call for help. Though Betty declined, he had no doubt that, at some point in the future, everything was going to come to a head. He'd be there to help Betty like he hadn't been for his wife.

Jonas set his glass down and stepped out onto the front porch once more. Best get back to work. The fence had needed repairing for a while now. He'd waited through winter because the ground was frozen. Thankfully, the handful of cows he owned were in the back pasture and he hadn't been worried about them escaping through the missing posts and wire out front. Now it was time to move the animals for better grazing. Fixing the fence was critical.

A noise caught his attention—a scream per-haps—gone before he could be sure. Jonas shielded his eyes against the afternoon glare and listened. Nothing but silence and then…a vehicle's engine firing down the road. He left the porch, his footsteps sure. Something wasn't right, and Charlotte was familiar enough with what Harley was capable of.

The frantic sound of a dog barking stopped

him cold. Harley didn't own a dog. This one had to belong to Charlotte. Had the scream he heard been hers?

Something inside warned that his concern was well justified. He didn't care if he had to fight Harley—he'd make sure Betty and Charlotte were okay.

Cutting across the property would be faster, but Harley had all sorts of booby traps set up along his property line.

Before Jonas reached the road, patches of bright yellow appeared through the leaves. The quiet of the countryside was broken by an approaching vehicle. Jonas ducked out of sight as the yellow Jeep eased past his position. Relief flooded him briefly before he spotted the driver. It wasn't Charlotte but Harley behind the wheel, an angry scowl on his face as he glanced over at Jonas's place.

Where was Charlotte? Jonas tried to untangle the truth as he watched the vehicle move out of sight. If Harley was driving the Jeep, he'd done something to the deputy. He wouldn't be driving her vehicle now unless he was trying to get rid of evidence of foul play.

Jonas ran toward the barn. He had to go after Harley and try to save Charlotte.

Though he hadn't been Amish in six years, Jonas still kept the ways, mostly because it was hard to give them up and he found comfort there. He didn't own a car. His only means of transportation was the horse and the buggy he used for longer trips to town.

He yanked the barn door open. Sandy, the mare that had been with him since the move six years earlier, glanced up at the commotion. The buggy would draw too much attention.

"Come on, girl. Time for a ride." Jonas worked quickly to get the saddle in place. Once he had it, he grabbed the rifle he kept in the barn and nudged the horse into action.

Sandy shot from the structure. Under Jonas's guidance, she galloped toward the road and didn't slow once they'd reached it.

A cloud of dust followed the vehicle. Through it, Jonas was able to see glimpses of taillights. He followed at a safe distance.

Harley had reached the road's intersection. Instead of turning, he kept going straight. The direction he was heading would lead deeper into the Beaverhead-Deerlodge National Forest, which was over three million acres, many of them isolated and uninhabited where few people ever went. Harley wanted to erase all evidence that the deputy had been to his place.

Jonas kept Sandy in the trees along the road. It made traveling slower, but he wouldn't be any good to Charlotte if he ended up dead.

The dirt road turned into little more than a path, yet Harley didn't slow down. He was driving deeper into the woods. The sunny afternoon was all but eclipsed by the trees, making it hard to see much. If it weren't for the taillights, Jonas wasn't so sure he could find the way.

After Jonas had followed Harley for a while, the Jeep left the path they were on. Jonas's bad feeling doubled. The route they were on led to a river that would feed into the much larger Madison River at some point. This was bad.

Harley drove the Jeep right up to the water's edge. The sound of another vehicle coming had Jonas urging the mare out of sight. A second later, the other vehicle, a small silver car, stopped a little way from the Jeep.

As soon as it arrived Harley swung the door open and got out of the Jeep. He didn't waste time rounding to the trunk. Jonas dismounted and moved close to get a better view.

Harley opened the hatch. Someone was in there. He had no doubt it was the deputy. A struggle took place as the female officer seemed to fight for her life. Jonas watched in horror as Harley pulled out a weapon and fired two shots. The fight ended.

Jonas stumbled backward and dropped to his knees. Had he just watched a murder? He gathered breath and realized if he could get to Charlotte in time, he might be able to save her life.

He prepared to remount and ride to her rescue. Harley slammed the hatch shut and returned to the driver's side. It soon became apparent what he intended when he shoved the Jeep into the water.

An instinct Jonas imagined came straight from *Gott* warned him not to leave his coverage until Harley was gone, yet the Jeep was now drifting away from the shore. The spring melts had the river rising. It wouldn't take long for the vehicle to be swept under the current and down to the bottom.

With his heart racing in his chest, Jonas watched Harley climb inside the second car. The driver reversed and drove quickly past Jonas's hiding place.

Jonas jumped into the saddle and dug his heels into the mare's sides. Sandy sensed the urgency and raced toward the river.

At this point, Jonas was almost certain he'd find Charlotte dead inside, yet he had to try to save her.

Jonas leaped from the mare and dove into the river that was close to overflowing its banks. The current was so strong it took all his strength to swim to the Jeep, which was being swept away.

A banging sound caught his attention above the raging water. Someone screamed for help inside. Charlotte was still alive.

"I'm coming. Hang on!" He grabbed the latch on the back.

"Hurry! We don't have much time."

We? She wasn't alone. Jonas thought about Betty and struggled with the latch while fearfully watching the rising water claim more of the vehicle.

When the door finally released, the relief was physical. The deputy's huge green eyes fixed on Jonas's. To his surprise she wasn't bleeding. Impossible. Had Harley missed in the struggle?

She climbed from the back of the vehicle and quickly went under. Before he could assist, she'd fought her way back to the surface and grabbed hold of the Jeep to keep from being swept away. "Help me get her out before it goes under. She's been shot."

Jonas' eyes widened when he realized the other woman wasn't Betty, but she was bleeding.

"I've got her." Yet getting the injured woman from the Jeep, which was now almost completely submerged, wasn't easy. The fear in the young woman's eyes urged him on. Despite being shot in the shoulder, she practically launched herself into his arms. Jonas dragged her the rest of the way from the vehicle, and she clung to him as he struggled to keep above the water while holding on to the Jeep that was quickly moving downstream. He could sense her trembling and held on tight.

The Jeep groaned as it shifted in the water and continued to sink beneath the surface.

"We've got to get her help. Do you have a phone?" Charlotte asked. "Mine was taken... I'm Deputy Charlotte Walker by the way, and this is Lainey." She indicated the woman in Jonas's arms.

"I remember you, Deputy Walker. I'm Jonas Knowles."

"It's Charlotte, and I remember. You're Harley's neighbor. The sinking Jeep is going to take us down with it. We've got to get away."

"*Jah*...yes," he corrected quickly. Even though he wasn't Amish anymore, Jonas rarely spoke to anyone. He'd gotten accustomed to using Pennsylvania Dutch in his thoughts and with his occasional conversations with Sandy. Letting go of the old ways was hard. "I'm sorry, I don't own a phone."

Lainey's hold on him loosened and she almost slipped into the raging water. Jonas grabbed her tighter, his attention on her face. "She's unconscious."

"Let's try to make it to the bank." Charlotte swam out in front of him. From where he was now, the riverbank appeared miles away.

"Did you see Annie?" Charlotte asked, glancing back at him. She seemed to be testing the depth to the bottom. "I believe I can stand up now. It might help fight the current." She appeared to plant her feet on the muddy bottom and he did the same. The water went up past her chest. Swimming against the flow of the water had been hard enough. Would walking be any better? He sure hoped so. They began to stagger forward.

Jonas realized what he'd been too frightened to see before. Charlotte had been through a battle, and it showed on her face. Harley had beaten her badly. Her eyes were swollen. Her auburn hair was pulled loose from her ponytail and soaked from the water. She'd taken a blow to the head. Blood matted the hair at her temple.

Anger rose inside at what Harley had done to her. He'd proven multiple times that he had no qualms about raising his hand to a woman.

Through his anger, Jonas remembered she'd asked about someone. Annie. Was there another woman missing? "Who's Annie?"

"My K-9 partner. She led me to Harley's."

Jonas recalled hearing the dog barking and told her, "She wasn't in the Jeep." He could see Charlotte was worried about her partner. After what Harley had done to her, Jonas could certainly understand why.

"What happened?" Jonas asked while keeping

a close eye on the direction Harley and his associate had disappeared. He took another step, trying to keep his balance while holding Lainey.

"I went looking for Lainey after her grandmother became worried about her. Dottie told me she liked to go to the Christian camp off your road."

He was familiar with the camp. Jonas spent plenty of time there pouring out his anger to *Gott*. "Dottie is Lainey's grandmother?"

Charlotte nodded. "Annie led me to Harley's house where I was attacked by a man in a mask." She told him about the Taser and then the beating. "The last thing I remember was being struck in the head." She touched the spot on her temple and winced. "From the glimpse I got of my attacker, I don't believe it was Harley, but I have no doubt Harley's in cahoots with my attacker somehow."

"There was another man who picked Harley up just now." Jonas hadn't been able to see him since he'd remained in the car while Harley did the dirty work. Jonas described the car.

Charlotte frowned. "It wasn't at Harley's house as far as I could tell. What's he up to?"

In the trees beyond the water's edge, a flash caught Jonas's attention, followed by rapid gunfire. The shots came from the trees near where Jonas had left his mare. Soon, galloping could be heard. Sandy was on the run, along with his weapon.

"Dive underwater fast—before we're hit. Go, go, go." Charlotte dipped beneath the surface. Bullets peppered the space around him as they swam away. Jonas quickly lowered himself and Lainey into the water and wrapped his arm around her waist. The frigid water woke her immediately. She fought to free herself while holding her breath. It took everything he could muster not to lose his grip on her. If she got free, she'd be swept away. And if he couldn't reach her in time, Lainey might die.

TWO

Charlotte spun in the water at the struggle taking place. Lainey had panicked. Charlotte swam back to the young woman and tried to calm her, but she was all too familiar with the cause of Lainey's terror. The younger woman had almost drowned as a little girl and had been terrified of water ever since.

Jonas pointed to the surface, and she nodded. Hopefully, they were far enough from the shooting to be protected from the bullets.

As she broke the surface, Charlotte searched around until she'd gained her bearings. The shots continued to pellet the water a short distance from her current location.

Jonas popped up, still holding on to Lainey. The young woman's fear didn't ease any by being above water.

"Look at me, Lainey." Charlotte got into Lainey's line of sight. The younger woman's breathing came in rapid gasps. She was close to hyperventilating. Lainey's frightened eyes latched on to Charlotte. "You're going to be okay. We're not going to let you drown."

Lainey slowly stopped struggling, her eyes huge and filled with tears. "He hurt you. He said you'd come to get me, and he hurt you."

Charlotte jerked back. Lainey had knowledge of her attack. A dozen different questions flew through Charlotte's head, but right now, keeping them all alive was her only concern.

"We'll have to make it to the other side." Which meant swimming across the river against the current.

Lainey immediately rejected the notion. "I can't. It's too far. I'm scared."

"You can because we'll help you." Charlotte glanced toward Jonas who nodded in agreement. "Let's get started." She searched behind them and saw that the car was now approaching the water. "Hurry." Jonas followed her line of sight. "They're going to try to get close enough to shoot us, and if they reach the shore, they just might accomplish it."

Charlotte carefully grabbed hold of Lainey's waist, avoiding her injured left shoulder. Jonas placed his arm above Charlotte's. Together, they swam for shore.

Charlotte's chest hurt like crazy where the bullet had lodged into her vest and would no doubt leave a nasty bruise.

Car doors slammed behind them, the sound reaching past her labored breathing.

"Hurry, Jonas," she said.

He jerked toward the sound of weapons being fired once more. Lainey screamed as several bullets came far too close to their location.

"We'll have to go under again." Charlotte didn't give her friend time to protest. Jonas released his hold on Lainey while Charlotte dove beneath the surface with her. While Charlotte was a strong swimmer, it took everything she could muster to fight her way to the opposite side after being injured.

She and Lainey resurfaced, both coughing up water. Charlotte searched the river for Jonas. He'd been right beside her when she'd gone down. Her heartbeat ticked off every second he was under and there were far too many.

Charlotte hauled Lainey to the shore. "Wait here." She dove back in and swam toward Jonas's last location. Before she reached it, Jonas called out. He was some distance from his previous spot, holding on to a tree that had gone into the water. She reached his side. They could exit the river here and walk back to Lainey.

Jonas swept back dark blond hair from his face. "Are you hurt?" Charlotte asked as she skimmed his face and realized this was the first time she'd really looked at him. His square jaw was covered in a beard only slightly darker than his hair. While he dressed Amish, she knew very little about them, or Jonas, except that the Amish settlement was some distance away and near the mountains. He didn't live there. She wondered why.

Once her parents had visited one of the Montana communities when she was a teen. They'd been told a beard indicated a married man, yet there hadn't been anyone at Jonas's house when she'd questioned him. Perhaps he'd simply grown the beard for protection against the cold.

"I'm fine," he murmured, his ice-blue eyes reminding her of the Montana skies on a snowy day. "I just had a cramp. Go ahead. I'll be right behind you."

Charlotte wanted to believe him, but the look of exhaustion clung to him. She spotted Harley wading out into the water. "They're looking for a place to get off a better shot." She found her footing in the water and helped Jonas out. Together, they hurried to where she'd left Lainey.

Charlotte dropped down beside the younger woman on the riverbank. Lainey held her shoulder and she looked as pale as a sheet.

Jonas sank to his knees near them.

Once she'd made sure of Harley's position, Charlotte leaned over to examine Lainey's injury.

"No, it hurts too much," Lainey moaned when Charlotte's fingers connected with the wound.

"I know it does, but I need to assess the damage." She glanced around. They were miles away from anyone who could help. It would be up to her to protect Lainey and get them all to safety.

Charlotte gently unbuttoned Lainey's shirt and pushed it aside so she could see the wound. Whether it was the cold water or something else, the bleeding had slowed. Still, the young woman needed more medical attention than Charlotte could give her. The medical kit she carried with her everywhere was in the back of the submerged Jeep.

She glanced down at her vest. It might help protect Lainey's injury from greater damage at least.

Charlotte quickly removed the Kevlar vest. The bullet lodged there was a reminder of how differently things could have turned out. Charlotte dug out the bullet and stuck it in her pocket to be used as evidence against Harley.

She explained what she was going to do, and Lainey slowly nodded. Charlotte cinched the vest as tight as Lainey could handle. "How's that?"

Lainey tested it out. "It feels better."

Charlotte smiled reassuringly. "Good."

"Did my grandmother send you?"

"Yes, she did. Dottie was worried about you."

Lainey nodded. "I'm glad she called you. If you hadn't found me, I'm not sure what they would have done to me."

Before Lainey could tell her what happened, Charlotte noticed Jonas searching the opposite riverbank.

She hurried over. "What is it?"

"I don't see them," he said.

Charlotte shielded her eyes and scanned the bank. "The vehicle's gone, too. We can't stay here, Jonas. They'll keep coming and eventually they'll find us."

This part of the landscape was at the far edge of the vast county she protected. Charlotte hadn't been to this area before, but Jonas lived close by. Maybe he understood better how to hike out.

"Is there a way back to the main road from here?" she asked him. They were all soaked. Even though it was springtime, the chill of winter still clung to the air. If they could keep moving, it would help put space between themselves and Harley, as well as fend off the onset of hypothermia with the chilly temperatures.

The taut set of Jonas's jaw was discouraging. "Not without crossing the river again, and that would be too risky." He glanced at Lainey to make a point. "Or walking for hours. If we

had a vehicle, perhaps we could make it sooner."
He shrugged. "There's a small group of Amish
families who settled in the valley many years
back. They won't have a phone, but I can bor-
row a horse and ride the five miles to the town
of Elk Ridge."

Not the news she wanted to hear but their only
option. No one was looking for her. She tried to
recall how much time had passed since she'd left
Lainey's home. Several hours. But not enough for
Dottie to have contacted the sheriff's department
yet. Dottie would be expecting Charlotte to call.
It could be hours before she reached out to law
enforcement.

The exhaustion on Lainey's face confirmed
she was in no condition to be exposed to the dip-
ping temperatures that would come with the approaching nightfall. Charlotte wasn't in the best
shape, either.

"Lainey's grandmother is the only person who
knows I'm out here and she won't call anyone for
a while," she told him without trying to sugarcoat
their situation. "What about you?"

"There's no one." His voice came out too
sharp. She focused on his closed-off expression
that warned her not to pry too deeply. There was
a story there that Charlotte wanted to hear, but
right now their lives were in danger.

"You don't live in the Amish settlement anymore." She'd taken a guess he'd once been part of it. The deepening frown on his face confirmed she'd guessed correctly. He didn't own a car or a phone. Why was Jonas—who clearly still dressed and lived like the Amish—not residing with those of his own faith? Had he been shunned?

"I'm no longer Plain." His chilly eyes warned he didn't want to talk about the reasons why.

Charlotte took stock on their current position. They had no weapons should Harley and his friend catch up with them. If they managed to reach the Amish community, at least there might be something useful to protect themselves.

"Let's head to the settlement. Is there someone there who would be willing to help?" The length of time it took for him to answer sent up plenty of warning signals. Something had happened to him.

"There is someone." He didn't elaborate, which added to her feeling that Jonas was hiding some guilt of his own. She of all people understood how hard it was to overcome, especially when it resulted in the loss of someone important…like losing Ryan.

Stop! Don't go there again.

She'd barely survived this last year while carrying the guilt that his death was on her. Ryan hadn't felt a hundred percent, but she'd asked him to help find Michaela and he had.

Charlotte pulled in a breath and let the anger and guilt—the self-loathing—go.

This situation was what she had to focus on. Getting Lainey safely back to her grandmother would only happen if she didn't allow herself to go down into a dark place again.

She thought about the attack at Harley's house and wondered who the man responsible for it was.

She turned back to Lainey, drawing the young woman's attention her way. "You said you saw the attack on me. How did you end up at Harley Owens's place to begin with?"

"It was awful. I was so scared." Lainey shuddered visibly at the memory.

Charlotte nodded. "I know it's hard, but I need to hear everything."

"It all happened so quickly," Lainey said, apparently struggling to keep it together. "Right after I'd left work." Her voice shook so much she was hard to understand. "I'd been driving down the road in front of the Quicken Mart when someone came out of nowhere and rammed me."

The accident was staged to kidnap Lainey. That stretch of road was pretty isolated with the exception of the Quicken Mart. Her kidnapper had probably been watching Lainey's movements for a while and figured out the best way to take her.

"He wore a mask," Lainey continued, "but I'd

seen a man with the same build in the store be-fore—several times, in fact."

"What did the man in the store look like?" Harley was well past fifty and overweight. His normal dress code was a stained white T-shirt and grimy jeans.

"Older. And he smelled. I was shaken up from the crash and disoriented. He came up to my door and opened it. The mask scared me. I knew something was dreadfully wrong." Lainey's voice sounded strained. "Before I had the chance to scream, he covered my mouth with his hand and jabbed something in my neck. I don't remember anything else until I woke up in a basement chained to the wall." Her eyes held tears. "And there's something else. I wasn't the only woman being held there."

There were other women trapped in Harley's house. The notion washed over Jonas like a night-mare he couldn't wake up from. Women were being kept prisoner right next to his place and Jonas had had no idea.

"Why do you suppose there were others?" Charlotte was asking.

Lainey wiped at her face. "Because I heard their whispers and then someone yelling. After that it got really quiet."

Jonas had no doubt Harley was involved in

something far more sinister than abusing Betty, which was dreadful enough.

"Then, another man came in. I didn't recognize him." She shook her head. "The new guy and the one who took me got into an awful argument. The second person was young and really mad. I believe he was in charge. I was so certain they were going to kill me right then except the one in charge heard a noise outside and went to investigate. When he returned, he said someone—a deputy—had come looking for me, and they had to get rid of us both. He apparently recognized you, Charlotte. The older man stuck something in my neck again. I woke up in the back of your Jeep next to you right before we went into the water."

And that's where Jonas had come in. He'd followed Harley and come across two attempted murders.

Though injured, both Lainey and Charlotte were blessed to be alive, but there were others in the house who might not be as fortunate.

Jonas couldn't believe he hadn't seen the truth that was right under his nose...just like he hadn't seen the seriousness of his *fraa* Ivy's condition until it was too late.

He should never have gone up to the mountain to trap on that final occasion. The baby was due in less than two weeks. He'd told himself

Ivy and the baby would be fine without him for a few days. But she wasn't. Ivy had been forced to harness the buggy alone in a snowstorm and drive it the five miles to her parents' homestead. By the time they reached the hospital, it was too late to save her and their unborn child.

Ivy's *bruder* had tracked Jonas down and taken him to the hospital, but they were both gone.

Losing her and their child had destroyed his faith and caused him to leave the Plain life behind for good. It was just too hard to live amongst his people and not see Ivy everywhere. Or endure the accusations from Samuel, his father-in-law, that were justified.

"Wait—did you hear something?" Charlotte was no longer pacing but listening intently.

Jonas stopped dead. It didn't take long to hear what she did. Someone was coming.

"They must have gotten across the river somehow. Quick—take cover." Charlotte urged Lainey behind some trees while Jonas looked for a sturdy enough tree limb to use as a weapon.

Soon, the noise became amplified around them. Multiple footsteps were moving through the area near their hiding spot. There were more than just Harley and the other man. Many more.

"Are you sure they came this way?" A male voice was close enough to hear clearly.

"That's what Harley said," another replied. "He

warned we'd better not let them get away or it will be all our lives at stake. One of them is a cop. Someone really screwed up by nabbing the girl."

"You know why he took her—she's pretty." Laughter followed. "He didn't realize she was friends with a deputy. He had a quota to fill."

Charlotte's gaze homed in on Jonas while disgust rose in his throat. They spoke of the young women they'd kidnapped as if their lives meant nothing.

"Yeah, well, because of his carelessness, we have to trudge through this stuff looking for them and it's going to get dark soon. You understand what we'll have to do when we find them."

"I, for one, don't like the idea of killing a cop."

Jonas's hand tightened on the branch. Despite everything they'd survived he hadn't wanted to consider that Harley was capable of murder, but these men hadn't held anything back. Once more, Jonas wondered what Harley was involved in and why he hadn't had some inkling on what was happening in his own backyard.

"Hey, it's us or them," one of their pursuers said. "I'm not going to die because Harley screwed up, and I sure don't want to end up in jail. If that happens, we're all dead men."

Jonas held back his shock somehow as the men began to clear out of the area. His hand ached from clutching the tree limb so tight he wondered if it might snap in two.

"I'm sure it's safe to move now," Charlotte whispered after what felt like an eternity. Lainey clung to her side, probably terrified those men would find her again.

Jonas slowly stepped from his hiding spot. The men were no longer visible. He'd heard two speaking but there were far more from the sound of them trudging through the woods.

"Which way?" Charlotte's question pulled him back.

Jonas could find the way to the Amish settlement with his eyes closed. He'd hunted this land since he'd moved here from Virginia in his late teens. After he and Ivy married, they'd settled into a little house he'd built for them some way from the nearest Amish neighbor because he'd been a loner at heart most of his life.

"This way." He pointed up ahead, grateful that they'd be heading in a different direction from those men.

Taking the lead, Jonas thought about what those men had said and couldn't imagine what terrible things Harley had going on at his house.

When Charlotte and Lainey caught up, Jonas voiced his concerns. "My guess is Harley is involved in trafficking young women."

Charlotte's lips thinned. "It's terrible to consider such things happening in our county, but I'm not naive enough to think it doesn't."

When he'd been part of the Amish community, he'd felt insulated from such things. Sure, they had their share of mishaps, usually involving the young people who went out on their *Rumspringa* getting into trouble, but there hadn't been any murders or taking of young women.

"I can't understand why I didn't see this," he muttered angrily. "I've lived next to Harley for six years now and I've seen the evidence he beats his wife—I've gone to the local police and reported it in the past many times—but I never thought…"

Charlotte tentatively touched his arm. "Why would you? These people are good at keeping secrets." She looked in the direction the men had gone. "What I don't understand is, why involve Harley? He's not the brightest person around and he's gotten into trouble in the past. He's on law enforcement's radar."

This was something Jonas didn't understand, either. He stopped suddenly as he recalled an incident that happened with Betty some time back. Jonas had heard screams coming from the house and had gone there with his rifle, determined to get Betty out of there.

She'd answered the door without a mark on her and claimed she'd seen a snake in the house.

When he'd offered to help her remove the reptile, she'd stopped him from coming inside. It was then he'd seen a man standing behind Betty. She'd claimed he was her nephew but there was something disturbing about him that assured Jonas this was no family member. Maybe the real reason Betty refused to leave was only in part her fear of Harley... Maybe she was more afraid of the man running the trafficking ring.

THREE

Charlotte tried to ignore the bitter cold settling in past her damp green sweater and jeans. It would only get worse with the coming darkness. She looked at Lainey who was shivering, her teeth chattering. Every little sound had Lainey jerking toward it.

"I hear something," Lainey said, her frightened eyes finding Charlotte's. "They're coming after us again."

At first, Charlotte thought it was just Lainey panicking until the snap of a twig beneath a footstep confirmed someone was close.

"She's right. Take her with you," Charlotte told Jonas and pushed them both behind a tree. There was just enough time to grab the nearest log before someone barreled from the woods and straight for her. Charlotte wielded the heavy log over her head and prepared to strike.

A man slammed into her before she could make contact. The force of his weight had her hitting the ground hard. Her head bounced off it several times. The log flew from her grasp. She was now in a hand-to-hand fight for her life.

"Where's the others?" The man straddled her before she could get on her feet.

Charlotte caught movement behind her attacker. Jonas grabbed hold of the man's collar and pulled him off her.

"He has a gun," she yelled and scrambled to her feet as Jonas and the other man struggled for the weapon. The unknown assailant shoved Jonas, forcing him backward. As he prepared to shoot, Charlotte leaped into action and struck his arm holding the weapon. The gun fired, missing Jonas by inches. If he got another clear shot, Jonas would be dead.

Charlotte grabbed the log and struck the shooter's midsection. He doubled over. She dropped the log and went for the gun, but her attacker wasn't letting it go. He struggled to get it into position to fire at her. In her peripheral vision Jonas had grabbed the log. He slammed it against the man's head before he had time to react. A look of surprise crossed the perp's face before he went down hard. The gun dropped free. Another blow to the head had him falling forward, unconscious.

Scrambling for the weapon, Charlotte grasped it and tucked it in her waistband before searching the man's pockets. He didn't have a cell phone, which wasn't a huge surprise. Many times, criminal elements weren't allowed to carry phones. Those in charge didn't trust the ones who worked for them not to be snitches.

She rose and faced Jonas. "Thank you for saving my life—again." A shuddering breath escaped her as another disturbing thought nudged at her to hurry. "There are others out here. They'll have heard the shots. We'd better get out of here before they come looking."

Jonas kept hold of the log while Charlotte went to retrieve Lainey, whose terror was written on her face as she stared at the person on the ground. "Is he dead?"

"No, just unconscious." Charlotte looped her arm with Lainey's and urged her away from the area as quickly as possible. "You should take the lead," she told Jonas. Almost like flipping a switch, the darkness of night descended. It would work in their favor to stay hidden but make it harder to see where they were going.

She worried about Annie. Was she safe? The last time she'd seen her partner was at Harley's. Had Annie managed to escape?

Jonas stepped out in front and started down the path, which was continuously rising as they neared the Roots—what the locals referred to as the mountain range that rose between the Jefferson and Madison Rivers.

"I'm so scared. I want to go home." Lainey gulped the words.

"I know, sweetie," Charlotte said softly. "I want to get you home, too. Right now, we keep moving."

Lainey tilted her head sideways. "I get so upset when my grandmother still sees me as a little girl, and yet now I realize how precious it is to have someone there for you."

Charlotte flinched as if she'd taken another blow. "You're right, it is." She thought about how hard it had been losing both her parents so close together. She'd found herself suddenly twenty-five and alone. Before their deaths, Charlotte had planned to continue her education and become a lawyer, but after her dad's death she'd needed to come home to the one tangible place left in a world crumbling around her.

After a while, Sheriff Wyatt McCallister, a family friend, came to her with a proposition. Join the sheriff's department and head up their K-9 unit because she'd helped her dad train dogs as a teen. At the time, she'd just been doing the next necessary thing, not realizing that setting up the newly formed unit would be the healing her heart needed. She'd gone through intensive training and then she and Wyatt had gone to an expert dog trainer, and she'd met Ryan.

She blinked back tears. Ryan's love had made

her not feel so alone. He'd given her something to look forward to. And slowly, she'd begun to dig her way out of the depression that grief had left behind.

Charlotte had a purpose—someone to care for her—life was back on track.

She'd taken charge of the K-9 unit and had loved everything about it. She and her then K-9 partner, Sage, worked well together. Charlotte had trained the other member of the team, Drew Hathaway. Sage partnered with Drew and Annie joined Charlotte…

And then Ryan died.

Up ahead, Jonas had stopped. Charlotte released Lainey and hurried to his side. "Do you see something?"

He turned those startling blue eyes her way. Instantly, Charlotte lost her equilibrium. The storm of hurt in his eyes, she was familiar with.

"No, it's just…" She stood even with him. He'd lost someone, too. She felt an instant connection with Jonas because of the pain.

At times, she'd wake up and think for a moment that Ryan was still alive, and she'd be happy. And then she'd remember, and the darkness would descend like a heavy cloud. Work helped. Annie was a huge blessing.

Charlotte jerked around and pretended to survey the settling darkness behind them. She wanted to look anywhere but at him, because like her, Jonas had to be seeing the depth of her hurt as well.

Lainey had sunk down beside a tree and was resting out of earshot, and Charlotte wanted to understand what happened to bring him to this point.

"Who did you lose?" she said softly.

He stared ahead. "My wife and child," he said in a rough voice. "I killed them."

She searched his face as a sliver of something unsavory crawled down her spine. "What do you mean you killed them?" Though she didn't know Jonas very well, she couldn't see him capable of murder.

"I was too busy being the adventurer to see Ivy was struggling with the pregnancy and needed me home until it was too late."

Relief swept through her body, replacing the unease. But it was followed by sadness for Jonas. "I'm sure you were only doing the best you could."

The smile that curled the corner of his lip held no real humor. "*Nay*—I enjoyed the solitude and the challenge of trapping. I told myself Ivy understood, but she didn't really. She needed me and I let her down." He nodded toward the settlement. "Her parents still live there. They've never forgiven me for what happened."

Now she understood why he'd stopped in his tracks. Why he was reluctant to return to the place where there were so many bad memories. Facing loved ones who blamed you for the death of your wife couldn't be easy.

She touched his arm. Felt the muscles beneath her fingers clench before he stepped back.

Charlotte cleared her throat. She'd crossed some line. "Sorry."

He dragged in a breath. "Abram, Ivy's younger *bruder*, lives in…" He stopped and gathered himself. "Abram and I were always close, but it has been years. Still, he was kind to me following Ivy's passing. Abram is a *gut* man."

Charlotte wondered about what he hadn't said, but now was not the time for questions when all their lives were in danger. "Then let's go to Abram's place." At least it might give them shelter from the weather and cover from Harley's men.

She motioned Lainey over and the three continued down the path. As they walked, Charlotte placed a protective arm around Lainey's shoulders. When she thought about what might have happened if Annie hadn't tracked Lainey's scent… If Dottie hadn't called.

Though she was worried about her partner, Annie could handle herself in just about any situation. But they were in real danger, and Harley was highly motivated to make sure they didn't walk out of these woods alive.

Everywhere he looked, he saw Ivy's smiling face. Six years hadn't been long enough to erase the good memories, or the heartbreaking ones that had destroyed the rest. Jonas had stood over his wife's body in the morgue and wept for the loss of the love of his life. That day, his life ended. He was putting one foot in front of the other—taking care of what needed to be done— but he was a dead man existing in a world he no longer recognized. He'd never share with someone else the love he had with Ivy.

When he'd first come to the Ruby Valley of Montana from Virginia, it was because he hadn't wanted to follow in his *daed*'s footsteps and become a beekeeper. Jonas craved adventure. Moving cross-country to the rugged land surrounding the Tobacco Root Mountains had certainly offered adventure and much more. He'd fallen in love with the remote community even though he'd only heard rumors about it.

The small Amish settlement, which butted up against the mountain, had lived up to everything he'd heard about it.

"How much farther?" Lainey whispered, breaking the past's hold. "I don't think I can go on any longer."

"She needs to catch her breath," Charlotte told him. "Let's stop for a second."

Lainey dropped down to the ground and placed her head in her hands.

The night made it impossible to see much more than his hand in front of him.

"How far are we from the settlement?" Charlotte asked from close by.

Jonas hadn't realized she was near until she spoke. There was something about this woman that made him uneasy. Not so much because she was in law enforcement. No, what troubled him about her was much more personal and something he wasn't prepared for.

"Still some distance. Abram's place is closer," he said in a gruff tone, then pointed down the slope they'd been hiking along. "Over there."

She followed his direction. A faint light, as if from a lantern, blinked in the darkness.

"How many families live here?" When he didn't answer, she prompted. "Jonas?"

He cleared his throat. "Five, at least, was the count the last time I was there. It may have changed."

Charlotte stared at him for a long moment before she said, "We'd better get going."

He shouldered past her without another word. A second later, Charlotte helped Lainey to her feet and followed.

As he neared the house that had once been his home, a lump formed in his throat that wouldn't go away. The lantern grew brighter in the window facing them. Abram was awake, but then again, it was still quite early. Darkness made it hard to determine time.

The last conversation he'd had with Abram stuck in his head through the years. Abram had asked him not to go. Give it time. Eventually Ivy's *mamm* and *daed* would see the truth. But Jonas had realized he wouldn't be able to stay there and carve out some semblance of a life without Ivy.

From near the barn, a dog barked. Jonas jerked toward the sound with his heart in his throat. Charlotte drew the weapon she'd taken from their last attacker and urged Lainey around the side of the house as the dog continued to bark, probably at their intrusion.

Footsteps came from inside the house. Jonas braced himself for the awkward reunion he'd never wanted.

The front door squeaked open—a reminder of the many times he'd promised Ivy he'd fix it. Some things never changed.

A lantern breached the door frame first, followed by a man. A man! The last time Jonas had seen Abram he'd been a gangly fourteen-year-old. This was no boy searching the darkness.

"Is anyone out here?" Abram's voice had gotten deeper as well.

Jonas stepped from the shadows. "It's me, Abram. Jonas." He reluctantly stepped up on the porch. The shock on Abram's face was no surprise. Jonas had told him he'd never come back here again.

Abram covered the space between them swiftly, holding the lantern high. "Jonas? I—I can't believe it's you."

Jonas wasn't sure what he expected, but when Abram enveloped him in a tight hug, it left him frozen in place.

"It's *gut* to see you," Ivy's *bruder* said.

Jonas slowly untangled himself. "You, too. I wish it were under different circumstances." He turned toward Charlotte and Lainey, who had emerged from the shadows, too. "We need your help." He introduced the two women. "Can we come inside?" Jonas glanced around uncomfortably as the dog continued to bark.

"*Jah*, come in and warm up." Abram's gaze swept over his disheveled appearance and then to the two women.

Charlotte and Lainey went on ahead while Jonas followed Abram inside.

His brother-in-law strode to the woodstove and stoked the fire before tossing some logs on top.

He straightened. Jonas noticed again how Abram had gotten taller and more filled out.

"I'm glad you're here, but curious as to what this is about," the younger man said.

Where did Jonas even start? It really wasn't his story to tell even. He faced Charlotte. "Perhaps you should explain. I still don't fully understand what we're up against."

She slowly nodded.

"Please—sit," Abram told them all. "You look ready to drop."

Jonas pulled up two of the rockers close to the fire and waited for Charlotte and Lainey to sit. He couldn't. Everything about the house remained pretty much the same as when he'd walked away from it, his life collapsing around him. He hadn't known where he'd go, only that he couldn't stay here any longer.

Outside, the dog had quieted. Charlotte's sweet voice filled the room. As she explained the twisted nightmare they'd gone through so far, Jonas leaned against the wall and found himself wondering about Abram's life. He'd be around twenty by now. Was he married? If so, where was his wife?

The expression on Abram's face once Charlotte finished reinforced how frightening the story was.

"This man Harley—he's selling people," his

brother-in-law said. The idea would seem horrific for someone like Abram, who lived a simple life filled with hard work and had only rare exposure to the unsavory world that existed beyond the settlement. One of the many things Jonas missed about this small, isolated settlement in the woods. That and the life he'd once had here.

Abram's troubled gaze found him. "What can I do to help?"

Jonas shoved off the wall and came to where Abram stood. "We need whatever weapons you can spare." In the light from the fire and the lanterns placed around the house, he noticed Charlotte's injuries, and Lainey's gunshot wound would need attending to. "Do you have something to bandage up their wounds?"

Abram swung toward Lainey. "You're hurt, too."

She managed a smile and told him what happened.

The horror on Abram's face was undeniable. "There are supplies in the kitchen and I have an extra rifle."

Jonas inclined his head. "Much appreciated."

Abram led him through to the kitchen where memories of the many meals he'd shared with Ivy crowded in.

"I heard you moved across the valley," Abram asked, pulling Jonas's attention away from the table he'd built for his wife. It wasn't much to look at but there were memories.

"*Jah.* I have a small spread across the lake. A few cattle." He shrugged.

"You always were *gut* with the animals." Abram brought out bandages and some strips of cloth. "You never remarried?"

Jonas flinched at the suggestion but managed an answer.

"She wouldn't want you to be alone, Jonas. You need someone in your life."

Jonas's jaw clenched. When he'd left Virginia, he'd been positive he'd live a solitary life filled with adventure until Ivy came along.

He stepped past Abram, breaking eye contact, and snatched up the supplies. "You haven't wed?"

"*Nay.* The settlement is small. There aren't many young women here. *Daed* tells me I should visit one of the other communities in the state. We have some cousins near West Kootenai."

Before Jonas could respond, Charlotte rushed into the room. "The dog is barking again." Her worried eyes locked with Jonas's.

Abram hurried past her. "I'll check it out. Lobo barks a lot. There are many wild animals in the area. It could be nothing."

Or it could be the danger they'd barely escaped closing in.

FOUR

The minute Charlotte returned to the living room, Lainey rushed to her side. "I'm scared, Charlotte. I can't go through that again." The fear in Lainey's eyes backed up those words. The terror she'd gone through at Harley's hands would brand her for life.

"You won't. I'm going to protect you."

Charlotte stopped Abram before he could leave. "The dog's barking might be him picking up the scent of another animal nearby, but we can't take such a chance." She looked to Jonas. "What if those men tracked us here? Can you and Abram stay with Lainey while I check around?" From the looks on their faces, no one in the room was convinced Lobo was worked up about a wild animal.

"Those men are heavily armed and it's obvious they want us dead," Jonas said. "If they're out there somewhere, you can't take them on alone. Abram will protect Lainey. I'm coming with you." The look of determination on his face assured her it would be useless to point out that she was the one sworn to protect those in this room.

Abram moved to Lainey's side when a noise outside came from close to the barn where Lobo was.

Charlotte trusted Jonas's skills and he'd saved her life more than once already. "We can't go out the front without being spotted. Is there a back entrance?"

Abram silently pointed to the kitchen and Jonas hurried toward it. Charlotte grabbed his arm before he could charge out into the night. He gave her a questioning look.

"We don't fully understand what we're up against. There's a lot of Harley's people looking for us. It's more than just our lives at stake." She tilted her head toward where Abram and Lainey stood watching.

"You're right," Jonas said with a shake of his head.

Charlotte slowly opened the door and listened. Nothing came from the barn, and she wondered if the noise they'd heard had been the animals stationed inside.

Jonas followed closely behind as she stepped outside. Charlotte edged toward the side of the house facing the barn while trying to keep the noise to a minimum. The pitch-dark and fog that had been gathering made it hard to see anything.

Keeping close to the side of the house, she eased to the front with Jonas at her six. There was nothing but yard between them and the barn now—a whole lot of open space should someone be hiding inside.

Charlotte pointed to the back of the structure. "On my word."

Jonas confirmed he understood while Charlotte counted off three in her head and prepared to cover the space that seemed miles away. "Go," she said and ran toward the back of the barn with Jonas attached to her hip. They'd barely made it a quarter of the way before multiple shots came from the front of the barn.

"Go back!" Charlotte yelled over the noise and slammed into Jonas as she turned to run. She fired several rounds, hoping to force the shooters back into hiding.

She and Jonas reached the side of the house safely and hurried along it.

"I counted three shooters," Jonas said, his intense gaze on her. "By now, however many others are out there will have heard the shots and come to assist."

Every word of what he said was true. But they were pinned down. The only way to get themselves, Abram and Lainey out safely was to take out the shooters.

She told him as much and waited for the truth

to sink in. Charlotte understood about the Amish being pacifists who shunned violence, but Jonas was no longer Amish. Did he still hold to their values?

"It will take both of us to manage this."

Despite their desperate situation, and no matter what Jonas's story might be, he had come after her when it meant risking his own life, and he hadn't backed down from the danger they'd gone through.

"I can't ask you to risk your life any more than you already have. You're a civilian, Jonas."

His chin lifted. "And you're alone without backup. I've come this far with you. Let me help you. You can't do this alone."

As another round of shots confirmed the shooters were advancing on their location, the decision was made for her. Jonas was right. It would take everything they could throw at the bad guys to get through this.

Sounds coming from the front of the house had her spinning toward it. Gun barrel flashes helped her pinpoint their location. She pushed Jonas behind the cover of the house and returned fire. "They're closing in for the kill."

"I'll circle around and see if I can sneak up on them from behind."

"No, Jonas." Before she could stop him, he'd disappeared.

Her attention was riveted back to the sound of multiple footsteps coming at them. Abram and Lainey were still inside. Should she try and get them out of the house?

A heartbeat later, it became apparent that the men were almost right on top of them. There wouldn't be time to get Abram and Lainey out.

Please *keep them safe...*

She glanced around the darkness for someplace to hide to give her the advantage. She spotted a small shed at the edge of the property and ran toward it. With her heart drumming in her ears, she half expected to be shot before reaching the shed.

Slipping to the back of the shed, she gathered in several breaths before peeking around the side. One armed man was followed by another. Where was the third?

The lead looked through his scope on the ground and Charlotte's heart sank. He had thermal vision capability on that scope. He pointed to Charlotte and Jonas's footprints.

"They split up," the lead said and then leveled the weapon toward the shed. Charlotte ducked out of sight. One or both were coming her way.

Lord, please help us...

The frantic prayer slipped through her head as footsteps crunched closer. She'd have to take her pursuers by surprise to stand a chance at surviving.

Charlotte kept her attention on the side of the shed. A shoe appeared. Time was running out. She had to act.

When the rest of the man's body appeared, Charlotte slammed into him with her full weight, taking him by surprise. She took advantage and smashed her handgun against his temple. He didn't have time to react before dropping.

The struggle captured the attention of his partner immediately. Charlotte grabbed the unconscious man's weapon in case he woke. She scrambled out of sight and prepared for another hand-to-hand struggle that didn't come. She heard a small yelp followed by a thud.

Her mind froze. Was it a trap?

"Charlotte, are you okay?" Jonas!

She slipped from her hiding place as Jonas came her way.

"What happened?"

He indicated the second man on the ground. "This one was coming for you. I was able to stop him before he could see me. The third man is gone."

"If I had to guess, he's probably warning the rest of his team. Which means we won't have long to get out of here." She looked back at the man lying near the shed. "We need to get these two tied up and out of sight in the barn."

Jonas approached the man he'd taken down. "Can you take his feet?"

Working together, they carried the unconscious man to the barn. Jonas found rope and secured him inside an empty stall. The man near the shed hadn't regained consciousness. Once he was tied up with his buddy, Charlotte hurried back to the house with Jonas.

"What happened?" Abram asked when he met them at the back door. "We heard shooting."

Charlotte explained about the two men in the barn and the third who had escaped. "We've got to get out of here before anyone returns."

"We can't leave them," Lainey exclaimed, and her troubled expression had Charlotte stepping toward her.

"Who are you talking about?"

Lainey was shaking. "The women that are being held." She was worried about the others. Lainey squared her shoulders. "Charlotte, I want to go back for them. I won't leave them to whatever fate Harley has planned."

Charlotte's first thought was to get Lainey, Abram and Jonas to Elk Ridge and the sheriff's office.

"Please," she pleaded. "They're scared."

Charlotte couldn't ignore those women or Lainey's pleas. "I'll go back for them," she decided. She turned to Jonas. "Can you and Abram take the buggy to Elk Ridge? Go to the sheriff's station and explain what's happened."

Jonas shook his head. "Abram, take Lainey and go for help. I'm going with Charlotte."

"No," Charlotte said firmly, "it's too dangerous." Though she didn't relish the thought of the miles of woods that stood between her and Harley's place, which posed all sorts of danger. There were people in them who wanted to silence her and anyone with her to cover up their crimes.

"I'm going," Jonas insisted.

Abram glanced between them before he went over to Lainey. "I can get Lainey to Elk Ridge safely." He smiled down at her. "I have an extra coat you can use for warmth."

Lainey nodded. "Thank you." Turning, she said, "And thank you, Charlotte."

"You're welcome. As soon as you reach town, call the sheriff and tell them what's happening and where we're headed."

"I will," Lainey assured her.

Abram added, "There are flashlights in the kitchen, and I do have some extra jackets in the closet. Take whatever you need." He slipped on his jacket, helped Lainey into one and ushered her outdoors.

Charlotte faced Jonas, saying, "I'll get the flashlights if you grab the jackets." He agreed and went to the kitchen and opened drawers.

Charlotte found a couple of extra coats in the closet. They'd help keep the cold and dampness away.

In the kitchen, Jonas held up two flashlights. They had both the shooters' weapons—she wished one of them had been carrying a phone, but she knew from past cases that only those in charge did.

Charlotte handed Jonas one of the jackets. He slipped it on and gave her a flashlight. Using them would draw attention to their location, but they'd still come in handy.

Outside, the sound of a buggy heading away from the house was a welcome one. She prayed Lainey and Abram would make it safely to Elk Ridge without running into trouble.

With Jonas close, Charlotte slipped out the back door and into the night. As hard as it was, she took a second to listen for any sound out of the ordinary.

"What's the best way to get back to Harley's from here? We can't cross the river again." At night and under the current conditions they'd both die.

"Give me a second. I'm a little turned around." He spun around while searching the darkness to get his bearings. Jonas pointed to the right of the house. "This way."

Together, they started walking.

"It's too risky to use the flashlights unless we

need them," Charlotte explained, heading into the woods. "How long will it take Abram and Lainey to reach Elk Ridge?"

Jonas turned his head toward a sound in the trees. Once he was satisfied it was nothing, he said, "Probably a couple of hours if everything goes well."

Charlotte understood what he hadn't said. There could be far more people out there looking for them. If Lainey and Abram ran into them...

"I hope that doesn't happen." She settled into his pace. "How long has it been since you left the Amish way of life?"

Charlotte glanced his way when he didn't answer. She was curious about him. Had she overstepped her boundaries once more? "Sorry, forget I asked. It's none of my business." She of all people understood some things were best left unsaid.

Jonas's clenched hand slowly relaxed. "No, it's okay. I left six years ago. Right after my wife died."

He'd mentioned his wife dying before. Charlotte's thoughts went to Ryan. She hadn't told anyone about her part in his death—that they'd needed his experience in mountain tracking to find a missing teen, Michaela Reagan. She'd called him out despite that he'd been sick and needed rest. He wasn't himself, and he'd taken a fatal fall.

Because of her, Ryan died.

"Ivy had complications with the pregnancy, and I wasn't around when she needed me." His quiet words pulled Charlotte from her own misery. He'd lost a wife and child. She couldn't imagine the torment he'd gone through.

"You couldn't have known she would have complications."

His laugh was bitter. "Regardless, I should have been there. She was noticeably frightened in the weeks before. This was our first child and she was scared, and I didn't do anything to help her. Instead of remaining at home, I just took off to the mountains to trap."

It was a useless and destructive game to look back and wonder what might have happened if one thing went differently. She of all people understood this. "Jonas, sometimes you can't help what happens. And regret will drive you mad..." Here she was telling Jonas it was useless to blame himself for what happened when she'd been doing the same things. Maybe it was time to accept Ryan's death wasn't her fault.

He looked her way. "That sounds awfully personal."

He'd shared about his wife. "It is. My fiancé, Ryan, died last year. It was my fault." She told him about the search for Michaela and her call to Ryan.

"I'm sorry. I remember when the young woman went missing, and later hearing about her death along with the death of one of the search and rescue workers. I didn't realize he was your fiancé."

Charlotte swallowed multiple times before she could speak. "Yes, Ryan's death was an accident, but Michaela's..." She shook her head, still refusing to accept the coroner's decision. "Her death was ruled a suicide, but I never supported it. According to Michaela's parents, she'd been looking forward to graduating soon."

"You believe someone killed her?" The surprise in his voice was evident.

She thought about what Lainey had gone through and stopped suddenly. "Lainey described Harley as the person who took her. She said there were other girls being held at his place. What if...?" She didn't finish because it was just too awful to consider. Was it possible that what happened to Michaela was connected to what Lainey and the other women had gone through?

Michaela's parents had mentioned she'd been scared of something before her death. If so, Charlotte was confident Harley was involved somehow.

She told her fears to Jonas.

"If this is the case, and Harley and whoever he's working for realize we've gotten away, he'll realize our first move is to call the police. Those women are in real danger. If he thinks the police are coming…"

Harley might choose to kill the women rather than have them implicate him and his crew. Charlotte started walking faster. "We can't let that happen." The guilt of not reaching Michaela in time still haunted her. They'd been only a matter of minutes away when she'd died.

Jonas's jaw tightened. "Harley's done a lot of bad things, but murder? I never thought he'd go so far."

"He's a dangerous man, no doubt. Still, I can't imagine he's the one in charge." In her opinion, Harley wasn't smart enough to run a human trafficking ring.

Jonas stopped suddenly and her thoughts shut off. "What is it?" she asked.

He faced her. "I heard something."

She focused on the darkness around them and heard it, too. Something was with them in the woods. Was it an animal or another type of predator?

He couldn't tell the direction it came from at first. The fog had everything distorted. "Whatever it is, there's more than one of them," he whispered in Charlotte's ear. In his mind that meant it probably wasn't an animal. "Let's head away from whatever is out there." He urged her along with him while praying the sound of their footsteps would not be as easily heard. At least the fog might help to distort the direction he and Charlotte were going.

They continued walking while he kept track of the noise. It was heading in the same direction as them.

"They're still coming," Charlotte observed. "We can't keep going this way." She turned to the left and kept walking. Jonas followed. The woods were thicker here. With the darkness and the fog added to the mix it was impossible to see where they were going.

Charlotte tucked behind a tree and pulled Jonas with her. When he would have questioned the move, she held her finger up to her lips and pointed to the direction of the sound.

Through the limited conditions, Jonas picked up movement. Dark shapes heading through the woods.

He strained and counted at least three figures. None of the men spoke. Had they been tracking Jonas and Charlotte all along? The thought was chilling.

The people he was observing suddenly stopped. He grabbed Charlotte's arm but there was no need. She'd seen it, too.

Both ducked out of sight. Jonas's heart pounded in his ears. Had they been spotted? He didn't even realize he was holding Charlotte close. It was just an instinctual gesture of protectiveness.

Seconds dragged by and then the sound of walking continued. He released a silent breath. Their pursuers were on the move.

He waited until nothing could be heard before he let Charlotte go.

She stepped back, searching his face. "We should be safe to move on." Her voice was somewhat higher than normal.

Jonas hadn't held a woman since he'd lost Ivy. That last time stood out like a painful reminder of all his mistakes. He'd held his *fraa*'s body at the morgue and cried until he hadn't been able to shed another tear.

And he hadn't since.

"I'm turned around. Do you remember the way?"

Jonas shoved his last images of Ivy back down where he kept his grief locked away and studied their surroundings. "This way."

As they started walking again, Jonas's thoughts ran rampant. He'd trapped the Roots during some of the worst winter weather ever. He'd been attacked by a brown bear and had a run-in with a mountain lion. Jonas had thought he'd seen it all. But what was happening now went beyond anything he could imagine.

FIVE

"Do you believe Harley has moved the girls by now?" Jonas voiced Charlotte's greatest fear aloud. "If he thinks the police will come looking for you, he might want to get them as far away from his place as possible."

Charlotte searched the darkness around them while suppressing a shiver. "I sure hope not. If we lose them, those girls could end up anywhere. Another state or worse—another country. These trafficking rings pick up and move quickly. Staying in one place for long means risking getting caught if someone notices an unusual amount of activity taking place where it shouldn't."

When she realized what she'd said, Charlotte turned his way. "You can't blame yourself for this, Jonas. Harley and his team are good at staying in the shadows. Not calling attention to themselves. Finding remote locations to hide the girls, like his house. You would have no way of knowing what was happening inside those four walls."

Jonas sighed. "Still, in hindsight, I should have figured out that all those vehicles I'd seen driving by my place at night weren't normal. If I'd investigated, I could have prevented what happened to Lainey or even Michaela. The thought that Harley might have killed the young woman turns my stomach."

"Don't take on the blame." Though Charlotte certainly understood the driving force behind his guilt. She'd been to speak to Harley multiple times. She was a trained officer of the law, yet nothing that would indicate a trafficking ring was evident during her visits.

"Does this stuff ever get to you?" Jonas asked quietly.

"Oh, yes. It's hard not to make it personal, especially when it is." Bitterness she couldn't stop crept into her voice.

"It must have been hard losing him in such a way."

She could sense him studying her profile, probably noticing the way her entire body tensed every time Ryan's name came up in conversation. The events of that day were still as fresh as if it had just happened. She wondered if they would ever fade enough where the good things—the sweet memories she and Ryan shared—could wipe away the hurt of all she'd lost.

"Ryan was the one person who helped me over

the pain of losing my parents so closely together." She told him about how both had died within a matter of months of each other.

"When I called Ryan to assist," she continued, "he'd been sick for a few days, but we needed his help with the search to locate Michaela." Charlotte was no longer aware of Jonas. It was just her and her memories. "I talked him into coming out and bringing his dogs because he was one of the best SAR trainers around and he understood how to work the dogs in the mountains." She stopped for a breath. Going on was hard.

"Ryan's last transmission was barely distinguishable. He mentioned he'd spotted Michaela—"

Getting the rest of the story out was hard.

"And then we heard his scream," she said in a voice barely audible. "We were able to pinpoint his location from the dogs' collars."

"I remember," Jonas said. "The incident was a tragedy only intensified by the death of Michaela Reagan."

"Yes. I never understood how someone as experienced as Ryan could make such an easy misstep like he did." She wrapped her arms around herself. "Ryan knew those mountains like the back of his hand. He could maneuver through them under any weather conditions or in the dark."

A pause. "Are you saying it wasn't an accident?"

Never once had she voiced her worst nightmare aloud to another soul before Jonas. The SAR team lead suggested Ryan's death was due to a mistake on his part because he'd been sick and not himself.

But what if it wasn't?

"I never believed Michaela took her own life." Yet she'd convinced herself Ryan's death came as a mistake because it was easier to believe an accident over something far more sinister.

Michaela was popular and well-liked. She was the star athlete on the basketball team, and her parents were loving. The only thing that stood out as odd was what happened about a week before her death.

"Michaela had called the station to report something strange a short time before her death," Charlotte said. "I was the one who was dispatched to take her statement."

Jonas's attention remained on her. "What happened?"

"This was about a few weeks before her death. Michaela called to report her friend Sasha missing. She didn't remember Sasha's last name but said the girl had invited her to a party at a ranch. They'd only met a few days before. Michaela said Sasha was friends with the owner. It was at night and of course there was drinking involved. Michaela swore she'd stuck to soda." She looked his way and saw the same doubts she'd had.

"Anyway," she continued, "there were lots of young girls there around Michaela's age but a few older men as well. Michaela said she got a bad inclination right away, and several of the men kept looking at her strangely. Before she could ask Sasha to leave, another girl came and got Sasha and that was the last Michaela saw of her. While Michaela tried to figure out what to do, she said she sipped on her soda and started to feel odd. Apparently, she passed out. When she woke up, she was alone. She looked everywhere for Sasha but couldn't find her."

"What happened next?" Jonas asked while keeping a careful eye on their surroundings.

"Michaela, though groggy, walked home and reported the incident. The ranch where she was taken had been abandoned for years and proved a dead end. Michaela did say something interesting, though. Sasha claimed to be seventeen—like Michaela—but she lived on her own."

"She was lying about her age. Why?"

Charlotte shrugged. "In light of what's happened, I hate to say it, but Sasha was probably working for the traffickers and brought Michaela there so she could be taken. Which was probably what happened to the other girls."

"This just keeps getting uglier." Jonas was clearly disgusted by what he'd heard.

She smiled gently. "It happens sometimes. The young women are older and not what their clients want anymore. Their handlers convince them to recruit more girls, probably in order to stay alive themselves."

"So why not take Michaela?"

"Because someone probably recognized her as being from a prominent family in Elk Ridge and figured if she disappeared there would be a massive search. Still, whatever happened that night set in motion the events that cost Michaela and Ryan their lives."

Jonas's jaw flexed. "I sure hope you're wrong about their deaths being intentional, because if not, then we have two murders associated with Harley so far." He stopped talking for a moment to listen before asking her about the day Ryan died.

Every second of that day was tattooed on her brain. She didn't even have to close her eyes to recall it. "When we reached the place where Ryan had fallen, the dogs were standing guard. They were faithful to him. Annie was one of them." Her voice became unsteady, and she swallowed several times. "She was the last dog Ryan trained and has been my partner ever since." She took a deep breath. "Anyway, while we were trying to bring Ryan up, there was a gunshot. I couldn't leave Ryan…" Sheriff Wyatt McCallister and several members of his team had gone. "They found Michaela nearby. Dead from a single gunshot wound to the temple." She pointed to the spot on her head without thinking. "The handgun was still in her right hand. There was gunshot residue of course. It was soon deemed a suicide."

"But you don't agree with the conclusion," Jonas stated. She shook her head. "If not, then someone made the scene appear like it was. Someone was up there with Ryan and Michaela."

"Exactly." Charlotte stopped walking. "I'm so turned around. Do you have any idea where we are?"

Jonas looked around for any landmarks and gestured where they needed to go. "I've spent a lot of time wandering the woods and countryside around my place over the past six years. I rarely sleep. At times I feel like a ghost flitting around searching for the person I used to be."

Charlotte felt like she'd found a kindred spirit in him. "I'm so sorry about your wife and child. Is this the reason why you left the Amish faith?"

Immediately, Jonas's guard returned, and she saw it on his face. The breakthrough they seemed to have made before vanished and she felt like a heel.

He cleared his throat. "We're not too far from

the Christian camp," he said without answering her question. She understood he didn't want to talk about the past. Talking about it was like reliving everything and she'd done that enough on her own.

This was the place where Lainey liked to visit. Charlotte remembered it vaguely from the one time she'd stayed there as a kid. "The fog makes it hard to tell where anything is until we're right on top of it." The damp from the fog also made the cold bone-chilling.

"Do you think Abram has reached Elk Ridge yet?" Charlotte asked because every second they were out here alone they were a target for Harley's people. By now, she was almost certain Harley's men would have found those three guys they'd taken down at Abram's place.

"He would have to stick to the buggy paths, which will slow them down. Still, we've been walking for several hours."

Charlotte checked her watch. "Exactly two hours and twenty minutes."

Jonas smiled. "Got it. They're close. If they haven't come across any trouble, they should be there in another fifteen minutes or so. At this time of the night, will there be anyone at the sheriff's office to help?"

"Oh, yes. Though Elk Ridge is small, Deputy Peter Sorrels is on duty along with the night dispatcher. They can have the sheriff and the rest of the team ready to roll out in minutes."

Jonas captured her gaze with a curious look. "You sound like you're proud of the work you do."

"I am. And I was so proud of my dad and the work he did in law enforcement."

An out of place noise had her stopping. "Did you hear something?" she asked. Her eyes darted through the darkness looking for danger.

Jonas glanced around. "I did. It's coming from behind us."

A second later, another sound was to their left, then to their right. With a sinking sensation, Charlotte realized they were being surrounded. The enemy had found them, and they were closing in.

"We need to get to the camp," Jonas whispered. "It's the only direction that appears clear right now. At least it will give us some amount of protection." Jonas leaned closer. "Whatever happens, we can't get separated."

She searched his face before nodding. "I understand."

Something he hadn't felt in a long time forced its way past the indifference Jonas normally used as a self-protective shield. He clasped her hand because he meant what he'd said about not getting separated. Together they ran in the direction he estimated the camp to be.

There was no hiding the disturbance their racing through the woods made or their labored breathing. They had to dodge trees that were impossible to see because of the fog. At any moment, Jonas expected to slam face-first into one.

As they ran, another far more dangerous sound had him jerking his head toward it. Gunshots. The enemy wasn't taking any chances of them getting away.

Both he and Charlotte ducked low. Keeping their feet beneath them with the momentum of running in a lowered position was nearly impossible.

After what his panicked heart deemed a lifetime, the shooting halted. The shooters either needed to reload or perhaps they thought they'd hit their target.

Jonas straightened along with Charlotte. As much as he wanted to ask her if she was okay, the sound of their voices would alert the enemy that they were still alive. He took stock of their surroundings and realized they were no longer heading for the camp. Jonas stepped behind a tree and whispered that they had to shift their direction slightly.

Charlotte pulled in several deep breaths before agreeing. "I'm ready." She spoke softly. "Let's keep moving before they find us." She'd told him about the thermal vision capability she thought those men were using.

If that were the case, then it wouldn't matter how far they ran, they'd be easy to track.

Stepping away from the protection of the tree and into the unknown was hard, but somehow holding Charlotte's hand made it easier.

So far, it didn't appear the shooters had caught their change of direction.

After covering some space, Jonas slowed to a fast walk.

Charlotte glanced behind them. "I believe we're too far away for their night vision capability to pick us up."

Still, Jonas couldn't get over the sensation of being hunted. Each step mirrored by the enemy.

Charlotte pointed. "I see something up ahead."

Jonas followed the direction of her finger. Several buildings emerged from the fog. He breathed out a huge sigh. The camp. Knowing there was a place to get out of the weather and take cover was comforting.

He remembered the place by heart. The first set of buildings were cabins where the campers bunked.

"Hopefully, we can find something to dry off with inside," Charlotte whispered. Both were soaked. Jonas stepped up on the porch of the first cabin and opened the door. The last time he'd been to the camp had been a few months back. He rarely went inside the buildings apart from the sanctuary that was in the middle of the site.

The electricity had long since been disabled. The camp had been closed for years.

Jonas clicked on the flashlight he'd taken from Abram's house. A half dozen bunk beds.

"There's nothing useful here," Charlotte said. "But on a positive note, there's no bad guys, either."

Jonas smiled. "We might be better off checking the dining hall."

She looked at him curiously. "You've been there?"

He nodded. "I've spent a lot of time here," he said in way of answer to her arched brows. "It's a little distance from here."

Jonas shut off the flashlight before stepping outside once more. The darkness descending almost felt physical. He listened for anything strange but heard nothing. If their stalkers didn't pick up on the change in direction and weren't familiar with the area, they might miss the camp entirely.

"I sure hope Abram and Lainey have arrived safely by now. We need them to bring help as soon as possible." Charlotte rubbed her hands over her arms. The cold seemed to pierce through the jackets they wore. "I hate being out here like this. It's impossible to see anything and we can't say how many men are out here looking for us."

The thought settled uncomfortably between them as Jonas kept close to Charlotte. They reached the large building that was the dining hall.

"The owners appear to have left a lot of the stuff behind when they closed the camp." He recalled the sanctuary was still intact. "Perhaps they hoped to reopen it sometime in the future."

Inside the dining hall were more than a dozen tables set up around the large room.

"The kitchen's through here." He'd explored all the buildings on his first visit. Jonas stepped through a set of swinging doors and into the kitchen.

Charlotte shone the flashlight around the space. "I could use something to dry off a bit." She began opening cabinets.

"There's some plastic containers over here." Jonas opened several before he found a roll of paper towels. "Here." He handed her several.

"Thanks." She dried off her face and hair. "I'm hoping those men won't be able to follow us, but if they do, they may realize we're heading back to Harley's. If the girls are still at the house, they won't be long."

He couldn't allow that to happen. "Let's see if there's anything useful here."

A thorough search of the rest of the structures produced nothing. The last building at the center of the clearing was the sanctuary. The minute he stepped inside, a sense of peace that had alluded him for so long returned. It was here every time he visited the sanctuary, which he'd done occasionally since moving to the area.

"I remember this place," Charlotte told him with a hint of surprise in her tone. She headed to the front where the altar beckoned. He followed. "I came here with a friend one summer when I was around eight. We had so much fun, but the best part was the final service. It was so moving. There were several kids who became Christians." A smile curled the corners of her mouth at the memory. Jonas couldn't take his eyes off her. She had a pretty smile. The thought was so out of place for him that it had him recoiling.

Ivy had been the only woman he'd thought pretty. He could still call up her face whenever he chose. Beautiful Ivy. Their courtship had been a time of getting to know each other, leading to a marriage of adventure he so craved...or so he thought. Looking back, he wondered if Ivy enjoyed all the adventures into the mountains he took her on as much as she claimed, or if she only wanted to please him.

When the baby came along, things changed. He'd had to grow up quickly. But he hadn't really. If he had, he would never have left Ivy alone so late in the pregnancy.

If he'd been there, he could have gotten Ivy to the hospital in time…his life would have turned out so differently. Instead, he'd had to bury his wife and his first child. As he'd stood over their graves, something had died in him that day. He'd left the cemetery a different person. Hope was no longer part of his world. Surviving each day without falling apart became his only goal. "Jonas?"

He realized Charlotte had asked him something. "I'm sorry."

Sympathy softened her face. "It doesn't matter. We should probably keep moving. I don't want to get caught here. I'd rather take my chances in the woods."

They reached the back of the sanctuary once more.

Before he could step outside, Charlotte barred his way. "Did you hear that?"

He did. Another heartbeat confirmed the truth. It was too late to leave the camp. The enemy had arrived.

SIX

Their only chance at surviving lay in their ability to stay hidden.

"Up front. There's a crawl space back behind the baptistery." Charlotte glanced down at her muddy shoes. "We have to take off our shoes. They'll follow our muddy tracks otherwise."

Charlotte slipped out of her shoes and waited for Jonas to do the same before heading to the front of the sanctuary. Two sets of doors on either side of the pulpit led to the baptistery, which could be reached by a set of stairs.

Charlotte chose the left-side door because if her memory served her correctly, it was the one that would take them to the crawl space. Her heart drummed its frantic beat into her ears. If they were caught, Harley's people would make them disappear just as assuredly as they would the young women she and Jonas were trying to rescue. To save their lives, they'd be forced to face those coming after them, and Charlotte had no idea how many there were.

She opened the door and went in with Jonas before carefully closing it without making a sound.

"There are the stairs to the baptistery," she said lowly. "The crawl space for doing repairs is past them. If you're not looking for it, you wouldn't realize it's there."

"How do you know this?" he asked, a frown wrinkling the spot between his eyes.

"My friend and I explored the sanctuary when we were here. If I remember correctly, it's creepy back there." Hopefully, too creepy for those coming after them to give it more than a cursory search.

Charlotte climbed up the set of stairs quickly. Once on the landing, the steps to the baptistery were right there. "This way." A thick green velvet curtain hid the crawl space where the plumbing could be accessed.

The space was small. Barely room for two people crammed in. If discovered…she didn't want to think about what would happen.

"I don't like it," Charlotte told Jonas.

"I agree. What's down there?" Jonas pointed to a ladder that appeared to lead down into nothingness.

She shrugged. "Becky and I were too afraid to investigate."

Jonas clicked on the flashlight and searched the shadows below. "It seems to be heading straight beneath the building." He turned her way. Saw the fear she couldn't hide. Dark spaces like what she'd glimpsed below were her phobia. "I'll go first," he said with a hint of compassion in his tone. "Will you hold the light for me? I can't see anything."

She took the light from him. "Go, I've got it."

Jonas tossed his shoes down and swung around on the ladder while Charlotte kept the light down and out of his eyes, directed at the rungs in front of him.

He slowly descended some fifteen feet until he was on the ground.

Before Charlotte worked up the courage to follow, the double doors at the back of the sanctuary were shoved open—with enough force to slap the walls. Charlotte jerked toward the noise. "They're coming."

"Hurry, Charlotte. It won't take them long to search the building."

She swallowed deeply and tossed the flashlight down first followed by her shoes. She swung her legs onto the ladder. The next rung was hidden by darkness and she froze. "I can't see my next step." Her voice rose an octave while her heart rate soared.

Jonas quickly corrected the issue.

Don't dwell on the darkness...

At the sound of Harley's troops storming the sanctuary, Charlotte carefully made her way down to the last rung. Jonas helped her off and she stood beside him breathing deeply to keep from hyperventilating.

Her attention went back to the ladder. "We need to get it down. If they find it, they'll surely search here."

"You're right." With Jonas's help, the ladder was pulled away from its resting place and laid out of sight. Both slipped into their shoes once more.

Noises from above told them that the intruders had reached the front of the sanctuary.

Jonas killed the flashlight and they stepped into the shadows, away from the opening overhead. Immediately, Charlotte took a step closer to him. The place gave her the creeps. She had disliked damp, dark spaces since she was a child, when she and a friend had gotten locked in her family's root cellar.

"I see something over there." Jonas held her hand as they moved farther along one of the walls. A small opening to the outside world had been blocked by a stack of bricks.

Before Jonas had the chance to grab the first brick, she said, "What if they're out there waiting for us?"

He stopped immediately. "You're right. It could be a trap. Let's wait for them to leave first."

Voices drifted their way. Charlotte couldn't make out what was said.

"Let's cover up our footprints so they aren't visible in case those men find the opening and look down."

"Good thinking." Charlotte helped him smudge their footprints.

While they worked, a door opened. Their pursuers were near the baptistery.

Both she and Jonas moved as far away from the entrance as possible. Soon, a light was flashed around the ground below and Charlotte prayed they'd done an efficient job hiding their footprints.

The light eventually disappeared. Darkness reclaimed the space. Once more, Charlotte edged closer to Jonas and waited.

"I believe they're leaving," Jonas whispered.

A light swept through the space between the bricks penetrating the darkness. Charlotte jumped back when it appeared to come close to their hiding place. After a moment, it disappeared.

Soon, there was no sound at all.

"I'm almost afraid to leave," she told Jonas.

"I feel the same way. Hopefully, they'll think we left the sanctuary and the camp."

She hoped for the same thing. They'd have to

be careful—Harley's people would know Jonas lived near the camp.

"Shall we move the bricks?" Jonas asked softly.

"Yes, I've had enough of this place." She shuddered. Clearing a way out didn't take too long. When the final brick was gone, there was enough room to move through the opening.

"Let me go first," Jonas said. He was being protective of her, and her heart softened in gratitude. But she couldn't let him. She was, after all, the one carrying the badge.

"I'm the deputy. I'll go first." Charlotte got down on her hands and knees and crawled out into the foggy night. She rose and scanned her surroundings. There was no sign of anyone close by. "It's safe."

Jonas followed her example then stood up, dusting off his clothes.

As they moved to the center of the camp, Charlotte spotted lights at the edge of the area. "Oh no." Her heart sank. She ran a frustrated hand through her hair. "We have to get out of sight." Using one of the cabins as cover, she and Jonas inched closer. "What are they doing?" she wondered aloud.

They appeared to have gathered there and were waiting for someone. "I can't tell." Jonas was close enough for her to feel the breath in which those words were carried. "But I don't like it."

She didn't, either. "I want to get closer and see if I can hear what they're saying," she said.

Jonas looked at her incredulously. "No, Charlotte. They want us dead."

She understood the risk but there was something more going on that she had to uncover. "I'll be okay. I'm a deputy. This is what I do." She searched his beautiful eyes before adding, "Wait for me here."

The words barely cleared her lips before he rejected the idea. "I'm going with you. We've come this far together. No matter what, we stick together."

Jonas witnessed the struggle taking place in Charlotte. She was worried about him.

"I can take care of myself, Charlotte, and those men are dangerous."

She slowly smiled. "You're right. We stick together." As she looked into his eyes, her smile faded.

Just for a second, the world around them and the danger close by disappeared and it was just two people looking at each other as if they'd discovered something they'd lost. Jonas wondered why, with this woman he scarcely knew, he felt a spark of something he hadn't felt since Ivy's death.

He stepped back, breaking the spell.

"Follow me and be careful." Her voice came out sounding nothing like her usual confident self.

Jonas managed a nod because his emotions were all over the board and he didn't trust himself to speak.

After another searching look, Charlotte slowly started toward the men while carefully watching each step.

Jonas's heartbeat drowned out all sound around him, and he wasn't sure if it was because of what lay ahead of them or what he'd just experienced with Charlotte.

They reached the back of one of the bunkhouses near the edge of camp. Charlotte held up her hand and stopped. Tilting her head to one side, she listened. "I still can't make out what they're saying." She pointed to a group of trees—all that stood between them and those armed men.

Jonas shook his head. *Too risky*, he mouthed.

But Charlotte was going despite the risk.

Before he could stop her, she ran toward them.

Jonas waited until she was safe before he snatched a breath and followed.

The conversation taking place close by stopped abruptly.

"Did you hear something?" said a voice Jonas recognized. It belonged to one of the men chasing them earlier in the day by the river.

Charlotte's wide eyes latched on to Jonas's.

"I don't hear anything." Another man Jonas didn't recognize sounded skeptical.

"I'm telling you I heard something. Go check it out to be sure." The first person appeared to be calling the shots.

Grumbling was followed by someone moving closer to their location.

Jonas instinctively gathered Charlotte close as if they could make themselves less visible that way.

Footsteps stopped near to the tree they were sheltering behind, and Jonas closed his eyes. *Lord, please keep us hidden.*

He kept his attention on the ground and saw what appeared to be the tip of a boot. *Stop, please, don't come closer.* The boot disappeared. Footsteps faded.

"It must have been an animal," their pursuer said once he'd returned to his people. "How much longer are we going to wait here?" He clearly sounded impatient.

"However long it takes!" the one in charge snapped. "He's supposed to call soon and let us know what to do next." Who was supposed to call, Harley? Or someone else?

"This is a waste of time, in my opinion."

"Yeah, well, there's a lot riding on Harley getting things under control and out of sight at his place. If the police come to investigate, we can't let them find anything."

Harley was moving the women. Would they be too late to save them?

Nearby, a phone rang. The leader spoke to someone briefly.

"Harley's not picking up his phone," the man in charge announced. "Never should have trusted that guy in the first place." A few unsavory words followed. "We still have a job to do. Find the deputy and the others. We don't need them causing a stink right now. Too much is at stake."

A bunch of varying opinions were expressed as the men talked over each other.

"Enough," the leader said. "Let's go. They aren't at the camp. Which means they're still out in the woods somewhere."

Soon the sound of multiple footsteps moving away could be heard. Jonas stood stock-still, too afraid to move in case it was a trap.

"Jonas?" Charlotte looked like she'd been trying to get his attention for a while. "We should be safe to leave now."

He let her go and stepped from the trees. The flashlights were some distance away.

"At least they don't believe we've come this way," Charlotte told him. "I guess that's something."

"Sounds like Harley isn't answering their

calls…probably because he's too busy moving the girls." Or worse. At this point, Jonas wouldn't put anything past Harley Owens.

"I sure hope not. Regardless, we must try and save them." She looked back to the flashlights and shivered. "Let's get out of here."

Crossing through the camp, they faced the woods that separated the camp from the road.

Jonas broke the silence, airing his thoughts. "With so many out here looking for us, hopefully we won't face any resistance once we reach Harley's house. Still, I'm worried about Betty. Where is she in all this?"

"A good question. I didn't see her before, but then I didn't make it inside the house. Is it possible she would have gone somewhere?"

Jonas immediately shook his head. "No. I'm certain Harley controls everything she does and who she sees."

Charlotte sighed. "That poor woman. Harley is a terrible person and Betty deserves so much better than him."

Jonas remembered the time when he'd heard Betty scream and gone to her aid. She'd told him there was a snake in the house. There'd been a man there who she claimed to be her nephew. Only Betty seemed almost afraid of him.

He shared the incident with Charlotte.

"Do you remember what the man looked like?" she asked.

"I do. He was close to my age, I'd guess, and he had short, dark hair and eyes."

"From what you've described it could be almost any number of people. And as we've established, this organization is much bigger than Harley. He's just a small cog and it sounds like his own people are turning on him."

Jonas agreed. "You're suggesting this ring is operating outside of Montana as well?"

Charlotte blew out a breath. "Probably all over the country if not internationally. To be able to do this, they'd need to buy off a lot of people in power along the way."

Jonas focused on her face. "You're kidding. It's hard to believe anyone in power would allow such an awful thing to take place."

"It's big business and generates millions of dollars each year. There are trafficking rings that operate within and outside of the US. They move women in and out of the country illegally. Sometimes using mules to cross the border. Other times, they fly them in on the pretense of working. Of course, it's just a cover for what's really happening." Even in the shadows, he saw how her mouth thinned. "I hate that such things happen to so many innocent girls. Even the ones who are saved, their lives are never the same again."

Anger rose inside Jonas. He couldn't imagine treating another human being the way these girls were treated. No matter what it cost him, he was going to do everything in his power to stop Harley and whoever else was involved.

SEVEN

Never should have trusted that guy in the first place...

Charlotte kept replaying those words in her head. It sounded like those in charge were losing patience with Harley. How long before Harley became too much of a liability to keep alive? Her fear escalated for those innocent young women trapped with men whose only concern was greed and keeping their crimes secret at any cost.

She voiced her concern to Jonas. "This has all the makings of a big operation. We can't let the girls get out of the county."

"I still don't understand why they'd enlist Harley's help in the first place. He's always been a loose cannon. It doesn't add up."

He was right. Harley had been in trouble with the law and was on their radar for abuse and petty crimes. She wouldn't have pegged him as being involved in something so much bigger.

Jonas stopped and faced her. "What if we're

walking into a setup? Because I have a bad feeling about this."

Fear shot through her limbs. "I hope you're wrong." By now, Lainey and Abram should have contacted the sheriff's department. Help would be on the way soon enough...*if everything went as planned.* Why were there no sirens filling the night with their sounds?

"Let's take a break," she said. Jonas had been with her through some awful things, and she hated that he'd been forced into getting involved. If something were to happen to him, she'd never forgive herself.

Jonas looked around for some place to sit. The only available spot was a downed tree trunk.

The dampness of the log soaked through her jacket and into her jeans. "I'm worried." She shifted toward him. He needed to hear everything on her mind.

"About us walking into an ambush at Harley's?" he asked.

That was part of it but not everything. "It's too quiet," she said, and his frown deepened. "Abram and Lainey should have reached the sheriff's office some time ago. Where are the sirens? We should hear them this close to the road." Where were her people?

"You believe something happened to them?"

"I hope not but we have to accept the fact they

may have been delayed or..." She couldn't say the words aloud. Couldn't think about having to tell Dottie she'd failed, and her granddaughter was hurt or worse.

"Which means it's up to us to save those women if they are indeed still there."

"Exactly." Charlotte hesitated. "Jonas, I'm worried about you, too. I've put your life in danger far too many times already. This is my job and I accept the danger, but it isn't yours and—"

"We've been over this already," he cut her off. "I'm not leaving you alone to face whatever might be waiting for us at Harley's. I'm coming with you," he insisted earnestly.

As she looked into his handsome face, something she hadn't experienced in a long time hit her like a storm.

When she and Ryan had first met, there had been an instant awareness. The attraction had grown stronger as they got to know each other. With Ryan's death, she'd felt as if that part of her life had died with him. But the way her heart was racing now just looking into Jonas's eyes... It was nice to have Jonas by her side. She hadn't had anyone to lean on like this since Ryan passed.

"Are you okay?" he asked, likely having seen what she couldn't hide.

Charlotte rose unsteadily and tried to put space

between them without being too obvious. "Yes, I'm fine. We should head out, though."

Jonas stood as well. "You're right. We need to hurry."

As they started walking again, the temperatures continued to plummet. "It's freezing out here." Charlotte wrapped her arms around her body for added warmth. It would be so easy to give up and just accept whatever fate that would come their way, but every time she thought about giving up, she remembered Lainey begging her to help the other women. As a deputy, she felt called to investigate.

"We're getting closer," Jonas said. The realization had her on immediate alert. The thought of going through another shootout was hard to consider, but they had to be prepared for anything.

She grabbed his arm as they neared Harley's house. Nothing but darkness appeared in front of them. "Hang on a second."

"Did you see something?" Jonas searched her face.

"No, that's just it. There aren't any lights on inside."

"Almost as if no one's home."

"Exactly. Wouldn't Betty be here?" Charlotte hadn't been conscious long enough to see if Betty was in the house, and Harley probably kept her living in fear and not asking questions. Besides,

Harley wasn't the man who'd attacked Charlotte. He'd been much taller and more slender than Harley.

"Stay close to me," she said because her gut warned they could be walking into danger.

Once they reached the structure itself, Charlotte debated on the wisdom of going inside without backup. Should they keep the house under surveillance until the sheriff and his team arrived? What if no one was coming?

She slowly eased onto the porch with Jonas following. A board squeaked beneath her foot, and she cringed before continuing. Jonas carefully avoided the step. With the weapon pointed in front of her, Charlotte moved to the door. Normally, she would announce herself before entering a house but right now they had the element of surprise and Charlotte wasn't officially here on police business.

Charlotte reached for the screen door and eased it open to a screeching noise that grated along her nerves. She tried the doorknob. It turned freely in her hand. Tension flooded her limbs. "I don't like this."

He was right there with her as she slowly stepped inside the house where she'd been a handful of times.

Jonas stepped over the threshold, leaving the door open.

From what Lainey had said, the girls were being held in the basement.

"We need to clear the house first," she told Jonas. "Which means we go through each room to make sure there's no one here."

He confirmed he understood.

Charlotte started on the first floor and checked each room using the flashlight to make sure they were empty. The house was neat and clean, likely thanks to Betty's influence. The kitchen was tidy. She felt the stove top. Nothing had been cooked there in a while. Charlotte couldn't get over the idea that something was terribly wrong, almost as if the house were staged. She'd overheard the men suggesting that the place needed to be scrubbed for evidence. There was no landline. She assumed Harley would have a cell phone, but wouldn't it be risky for connecting with his cohorts?

An uneasy tension settled between her shoulder blades.

Once the second floor was cleared, Charlotte and Jonas went back down to the kitchen where the door to the basement was located.

Outside, nothing but silence. The sirens and flashing lights she'd prayed for didn't come.

His heart echoed every step leading down to the basement. Charlotte held the flashlight, shining it around. The room was surprisingly uncluttered. Only a few pieces of furniture had been stored down here. Nothing more.

Jonas's heart plummeted. "Now what?"

Disappointment was clear on Charlotte's face. "I can't believe it. This is Harley's house. Those men said he was getting the girls out of sight. Where are they?" She spun around the room. "Is there another building we missed?"

"Wait, what's that?" Jonas spotted something over in the corner of the room and picked it up.

"It's a denim jacket." Charlotte took the garment from him. "Betty's?"

"Doubtful. I've never seen her wear anything like it." It had been hand stitched with a flower design in brightly colored threads.

She turned the jacket over and looked inside. "It's a size two. I don't believe it would fit Betty. It could belong to one of the girls. I need Annie. She could help us locate the owner." Her expression saddened. "I hope she's okay."

"She's obviously a smart dog. Is it possible she's still searching for Lainey?" He could tell she wasn't fully convinced. Charlotte flashed the light all around once more and he followed the beam. "I don't see anything else. Harley doesn't have a garage. The house is it."

"We're too late."

Jonas tried to make sense of it. "This isn't the

best spot to hide anyone. If Harley is involved, it's the first place law enforcement would look."

"So, if not here, then where would he take them?"

Realization dawned within him and he slapped his palm against his forehead. "I don't understand why I didn't think of this earlier."

Charlotte stepped forward. "What?"

"I still go trapping in the wintertime. The last time I did—a few months back—I ran into Harley up in the mountains. He seemed surprised to see me."

"What was he doing up there?"

Jonas had wondered as much himself. "He seemed cagey as all get-out."

"He was hiding something," she concluded.

"Those were my thoughts. At the time I had no idea the scope of what Harley was capable of." He shook his head. "Anyway, I asked him why he was in the mountains in the wintertime because Harley isn't a hunter or a trapper."

Charlotte's brow creased. "He was doing something illegal."

"I have no doubt about it now. Harley told me he owned a place up there and came there to get away from time to time."

Charlotte's frown deepened. "That can't be the case."

"My thoughts, too. It could belong to one of

his criminal buddies. I'm guessing Harley left the men searching for us and ditched the person who picked him up at the river so he could move the women. He'd certainly have enough time by now."

"You're right. We've been looking at the wrong house." Her shoulders slumped. "And we've wasted valuable time trying to get here."

Jonas felt like a heel for not remembering sooner. "If we don't find those young women soon, I can't even imagine the world they'll be subject to."

She searched his face. "But how? Do you have any idea which place is his?"

He did. "I can find it. There are only a few places on the mountain, and most are used for trapping. Harley couldn't take the girls there because those cabins are usually one room and small." Jonas remembered one house in particular that was much bigger. He told her about it. "I always wondered who it belonged to because it didn't fit with the rest up there. I'm guessing it's the one Harley claimed was his."

"Let's go." Charlotte started up the stairs. A second later, Jonas caught up with her.

Charlotte suggested they find some dry clothes to change into before heading up to the mountains.

"I think I saw some in the bedroom." They

returned to the room she assumed Betty shared with Harley, and Charlotte dug through the closet until she found something that would work for both her and Jonas. They changed in separate rooms and stepped into the hallway a couple minutes later. Harley's jeans were too short for him, and Charlotte suppressed a grin.

"Not exactly a good fit, but they're dry," he said in answer to her obvious amusement. They went back downstairs, where Charlotte stuffed their damp clothes in a trash bin.

Before they reached the front door, a set of flashlights appeared in the woods in front of the house.

Charlotte ducked away from the window that ran alongside the door. "Someone's out there."

Jonas watched the lights from the corner of a glass pane. "They're coming this way. The back door."

He ran for the kitchen where he'd noticed a second entrance. Before he stepped out into the darkness, Jonas carefully scanned the surroundings to make sure there was no one coming up on them. He and Charlotte stepped out and closed the door as quietly as possible. He didn't want to give those men approaching a heads-up. Unfortunately, as careful as both were trying to be, Harley's back porch was a mess and several of the boards creaked beneath their feet.

"Run!" Charlotte whispered. Both jumped from the porch and raced toward the woods in front of them.

"That's far enough. Stop where you are." A flashlight beam pinned them in place. Two of Harley's people headed their way.

"Well, well. This is a lucky surprise. Where's Harley?" one man said.

The person without the light immediately sounded the alert to the others who were close.

Shocked, Jonas jerked his head toward Charlotte.

"We can't let them take us," she said under her breath. He understood what she meant. They'd have to fight for freedom.

As the two approached, Jonas whirled around and fired. Both men ducked. Jonas ran after the one with the light and slammed into him hard with all his weight. It took everything Jonas could muster to fend the man off and keep from being shot. Out of the corner of his eye, he saw that Charlotte was struggling with the second man. Voices of the others who were with them drifted his way. They were almost out of time.

Jonas slugged his attacker hard, but the man just kept coming, matching him fist for fist. Jonas finally managed to get his weapon in a position to strike the man hard. It was enough to drop him to his knees. He fell forward and sprawled on the ground unconscious. Jonas grabbed his weapon.

Charlotte!

The second man was about to shoot. Jonas ran toward the nightmare unfolding. A rustling noise nearby had the shooter pausing.

A dog raced from the woods before he had the chance to react. This was Annie, Charlotte's K-9 partner. The man shot at the animal and missed. Annie grabbed hold of his arm and latched on tight. Cursing, the man tried to shake the dog off but couldn't.

The unconscious man woke and scrambled to his feet then ran toward the woods. Jonas fired but missed.

The second armed soldier kicked Annie hard. The dog let go.

"We have to get out of here," Charlotte yelled to Jonas. "Come, Annie." With the dog leading the way, they all ran for the woods while the remaining attacker shot at them.

By *Gott*'s hand they'd escaped unscathed.

"Don't stop," Charlotte told him as they continued running as fast as possible to put distance between themselves and the house.

Jonas kept careful watch behind. This direction would take them deeper into the woods. There wasn't another house past Harley's. At some point, they'd have to change direction.

"Why aren't they coming after us?" Charlotte slowed to a fast walk with the dog keeping pace.

He stopped and looked the way they'd come. "I can't say. The one guy saw which way we went but didn't follow."

"They weren't there for us."

"Harley." Their attacker had asked where Harley was and, in the woods earlier, Jonas overheard one saying Harley wasn't picking up. "They were sent to find him."

"Exactly. He's really made someone angry." Charlotte focused on the dog and did a quick exam. Jonas noticed blood on Annie's head. "She has a small cut and there's a bump. It looks as if she's been struck by something."

"Probably when you were attacked earlier."

"Possibly." She gave the dog a hug and then brought out the denim jacket. "Search, Annie."

The dog immediately sniffed the ground before picking up a scent. She started for the front of the house. Charlotte stopped her. "We can't risk her running into danger. Would Harley be able to get the women to the house by vehicle?"

"It would have to be four-wheel drive. It's rugged up there." As happy as Jonas was that the dog was found, he still didn't trust those men not to come after them. "Let's keep moving."

Charlotte kept a close eye on the dog as they

moved through the woods at the side of the house. "Does Harley own a Jeep or a four-wheeler?"

"Not that I recall. Look." He pointed to the house. "They're inside now." The men didn't appear to be too concerned about Charlotte and Jonas. They'd come for Harley.

Annie sniffed around the ground without picking up a scent.

"After you cross the mountains, there's a valley below that's sparsely populated," Charlotte said. "It would provide a good passage to move the girls without being spotted."

Jonas hadn't thought about it before. "Makes sense. But I wouldn't consider it ideal in the winter months. The snow gets deep up there. You'd have to have a special type of machine in order to travel through it."

"You're right. Unless Harley was up to something besides trafficking young women."

"Like what?" Jonas watched her closely.

"Possibly weapons smuggling or a dozen different scenarios just as bad."

Disgust rose inside Jonas. "I always thought Harley was a bad person, but I had no idea how bad."

Charlotte glanced behind them. "There's no sign we're being followed."

"To be safe, we should avoid the camp. As it is, it will be several hours before we reach the mountains. Avoiding the camp won't cause us much more of a delay. The way I'm going to take us would be accessible by a four-wheel drive vehicle. If we can pick up Harley's trail again, Annie can get back on the kidnapped woman's scent."

"I hope so." Charlotte bit down on her bottom lip. "To be honest, if I never see that camp again, it will be too soon."

Jonas smiled. He certainly understood. Their last visit had been terrifying.

"Still, I'm worried about how we'll let my people know where we are," Charlotte said. "They'll be expecting us at Harley's house, and we have no way of getting word to them about the change in direction. They could be walking into a dangerous situation if those men are still around."

Their attackers were willing to take anyone out to accomplish their mission. If cornered by law enforcement, he couldn't imagine the carnage. "I don't remember any *Englischer* houses between here and the mountains where we can use their phones."

Charlotte frowned. "Annie's collar has a tracking device made into it."

"Would your team automatically consider checking the location of the dog?"

"Probably…but we can't afford to take the chance." She stopped walking. "We need to leave word for them somewhere they'll think to check when they don't find us at Harley's."

"My house," he answered. "It's closer."

"Yes! My place is miles away by vehicle—which we don't have. Abram and Lainey know you're with me. If we circle back to your place and leave a note, perhaps it will be found by the sheriff's department."

"Or by those men. We could be leading them to where we're going."

She didn't deny it. "That's possible, too."

Did they dare take the chance that those at Harley's wouldn't check his home? "We have to try," he told her because he had a bad feeling about Abram and Lainey. With so many men combing the woods, had the two managed to reach help? If so, why was it taking so long for help to reach them?

With Annie glued to Charlotte's side, they made a wide berth around Harley's place. The miles covered since he'd last left his house weighed on his exhausted limbs.

His house appeared through the fog. After checking for any sign of a vehicle moving their way, Jonas crossed the road with Charlotte and the dog.

As he neared the house, the hackles at the back of his neck stood at attention. Something felt off.

"Let's take a detour," he whispered and guided

her toward the barn. Once they were inside, his fears didn't ease any by the realization that his horse hadn't returned.

"Sandy's not here."

Charlotte studied his face. "Who's Sandy?"

"My mare. I rode her to the river. The shooting spooked her, but she normally would return home." He turned toward the door he'd left open. "She always comes home."

Charlotte followed his gaze. "You believe someone took her?"

He didn't know what he thought. He faced Charlotte again. "Stay here. Let me slip around the back and see if I can get a good look inside."

Charlotte immediately shook her head. "It's too dangerous. I'm coming with you."

It would be pointless to try and change her mind. Jonas pointed to the side door. "That way."

Annie fell into step while Jonas eased toward the back of the barn and prayed if his hunch was true, those men wouldn't be looking for them.

Once they were even with the house, he quickly crossed around back with Charlotte and the dog.

The window at the back of the house looked out from the kitchen. Inside was darkness. Jonas stepped close and tried to see in.

"Do you see anything?" Charlotte whispered.

He leaned closer. A shadow moved inside, and then he was looking into the face of the enemy.

EIGHT

"Go, go, go!" Jonas yelled. He peeled off around the side when a shot shattered the window they had just been looking through.

Another round of shots followed in rapid succession.

Charlotte charged through the night, grasping for Jonas's hand. She needed to know they were all moving together.

"Which way?" she asked, because in the dark and under these weather conditions everything looked the same.

"Left."

They raced behind the barn and kept going while the sound of pursuit could be heard.

"They're coming. Don't stop," Jonas told her.

He was their only chance at survival. She knew he understood the layout of the land far better than these men after them.

They crossed the road. Charlotte glanced

around and was happy to see Annie right at their heels.

Once they reached the other side, Jonas didn't slow down. They charged through the woods, fighting back the dense underbrush Charlotte had faced before. The cold burned her lungs.

Behind them, what sounded like several men were searching Jonas's property. Those at Harley's house would join the search soon enough. They couldn't afford to stop.

Charlotte lost her footing and almost went down. She would have if it weren't for Jonas's hold on her.

After they'd been running for a long time, Jonas stopped long enough to listen. "I don't hear them yet."

Which meant they had the advantage for the moment.

"Let's see if we can get back on the four-wheeler path," Charlotte said, and they started walking at a fast pace. Her worst fear was that the others were heading their way to cut them off. She said as much to Jonas.

"I'm worried, too," he replied. "Yet they don't know where we're going, which will work to our favor." He looked behind them. "If we keep going, we'll reach the camp, which I don't think is wise." He pointed to the left. "Best to take a little longer to get there and get there alive."

A chill sped down her spine at those words. She was struggling to breathe normally after their race for freedom. "Are we safe slowing down a bit?"

Jonas must've noticed her struggle. "We should be." He slowed his steps to match hers. "Why were they at my house?"

Charlotte was convinced they were expecting them to come back to Jonas's at some point and said so.

"Which is probably why they took Sandy," Jonas decided. "To keep me from using her to ride for help."

"Exactly." Charlotte peeked over her shoulder. If Harley's people realized where they were heading, they'd move the girls for sure, if they hadn't already.

Once they had traveled for some time, Jonas stopped and knelt beside a set of tracks. "Look. These appear too small to belong to a Jeep and you'd never get a pickup through here. It could be one of those side-by-sides."

Charlotte glanced at the tracks—they certainly could belong to an off-road utility vehicle. She took out the jacket once more. Annie sniffed the garment and then the air in several directions before taking off. "She's found the scent."

While they followed Annie, her thoughts kept returning to Lainey and Abram. Was she worried for no reason? Perhaps they'd just been delayed.

"Whatever happened, Lainey is with Abram. He'll protect her," Jonas said as if reading her troubled thoughts.

"I hope you're right, but neither of them has been up against anything like this."

"Abram is smart and knows these woods well," Jonas said. "The best way we can help right now is to find those women and get them to a safe location before they're moved or hurt. If Harley and his people were responsible for killing Ryan and Michaela, they must be stopped."

His words had her slowing in her tracks, but he was right. For so long, she hadn't wanted to consider that Ryan might have been met with foul play or was even murdered, but the question was always there in the back of her mind. The thought of someone killing him and Michaela to protect their crimes was unthinkable. "Whatever happened a year ago started with Michaela." Charlotte glanced sideways at Jonas and saw him agree.

"It sounds like it has everything to do with what happened to her friend Sasha and that party."

Charlotte frowned. "Yes. But Michaela didn't recognize any of the men there—at least that's what she claimed."

Jonas shook his head. "It doesn't make sense.

Sasha made a mistake with Michaela, just like Harley did with Lainey."

It sickened Charlotte to consider what Harley had planned for Lainey before she was introduced into the sex trafficking world. "Sasha and now Harley screwed up and put a spotlight on the organization. Ryan's death was made to look like a fall to cover up something he probably saw that night." Her stomach clenched as she said the words aloud. "Michaela's was staged to look like a suicide. I don't know what they'd do to Lainey if they catch her." Or them. All she knew for certain was they wouldn't live to tell their side of the story.

A noise up ahead had Annie investigating. The dog soon lost interest and retraced her tracks.

Charlotte tried to relax. "How long have you lived in this area?" she asked, not only because she was curious about him, but also because she had to find something for her brain to fix on other than the danger all around them.

He lowered his head. "I moved here from Virginia when I was seventeen."

Charlotte was surprised to hear he'd come from out east. "That's a big move for someone so young."

He attempted a smile. "I guess. Strangely, I never hesitated. My father was a beekeeper like his father before him."

She looked at him, silently inviting him to tell her more. "But you didn't want to follow in the family business."

"I didn't. In fact, I couldn't imagine anything more boring to be honest with you." He laughed before continuing. "I'd heard about Montana and the mountains. Seen pictures of them. I couldn't wait to see them for myself."

"And did they live up to what you imagined?" She'd lived here all her life. Most times, the mountains were just something in the distance and easy to take for granted.

"Yes, they did," he said with awe in his voice. "I loved everything about them. For the first year, I traveled around the different communities in Montana before settling here."

"And you found the settlement?" She watched Annie weave her way through the tall brush.

"I did. I went to work for Ivy's *daed*. In my spare time, I taught myself how to trap and made a decent living at it."

"And you and Ivy?" She waited to hear their love story.

"I actually loved her the moment I saw her, only she was fifteen at the time and her *daed* wanted her to wait for a couple of years before marrying." His mouth quirked. "I was happy to wait for her. I loved her so much."

Her thoughts returned to Ryan. She'd felt the

same way the first time they met. When he asked her out, she thought she was the luckiest person alive. In typical Ryan fashion, he'd invited her to join in the dog training. She'd gotten to see him in action. The way he interacted with the animals. It was a beautiful thing.

"While I waited, I built the house where Abram now lives."

Charlotte hadn't realized that. No wonder it seemed hard for him to go there. "Abram lives in your old house?"

He jerked his head in answer. "After Ivy died, I could no longer stay Amish. I'd failed Ivy. Let my own desires take precedence over her needs."

"Oh, Jonas." Charlotte hated that he blamed himself. The "what if" game was futile and there were no winners. "I felt the same way about what happened to Ryan," she reminded him softly, capturing his attention.

He shook his head. "Ryan understood the dangers of going up when he wasn't a hundred percent."

She stopped walking and faced him. "Take your own advice, Jonas." He looked deep into her eyes and smiled slightly.

"It's hard. My head tells me I couldn't have predicted what happened to Ivy and yet my heart…"

She stepped closer and placed her hands on his shoulders. "I understand exactly what you mean, but I believe both Ivy and Ryan wouldn't want us to keep blaming ourselves forever for what happened."

His eyes held hope. "I want to let it go. It's such a heavy burden to carry."

She did something that was as much a surprise to her as it was to Jonas. Charlotte wrapped her arms around his waist and tugged him close. She held him and could feel his body quaking.

"This is something we can work on together." She wanted to try to move past the guilt. She had to. If she didn't, she'd spend the rest of her life living in regret.

Jonas pulled away and searched Charlotte's face. For reasons he couldn't let himself explore, going through this with Charlotte made him feel better.

"We should probably keep going," he said softly, but he didn't want to. More than anything he wanted this to be over.

And then...

Best not to go there. He couldn't lose someone else that he cared about. Ivy and the baby had almost broken him.

Charlotte let him go and stepped back. "You're right." She shifted the conversation back to the task at hand. "I promised Lainey's grandmother I would bring her home safely, and I would hate to put Abram's life in jeopardy after he went out of his way to assist us."

"Abram's smart." Jonas searched the woods around them. He couldn't explain why he was so much more on edge than before except because of what they'd gone through.

"I see something up ahead." Charlotte pointed.

Through the darkness and fog he was able to make out a dark shape. "It looks like some type of shelter."

Annie reached the structure when it dawned on Jonas what it was. "That's one of the forest service's lookout stations. They have several around. During the fire season, they're manned to help prevent fires."

The dog waited near the entrance.

Jonas opened the door, and he, Charlotte and the dog went inside. He'd explored this station as well as some of the others before. The building consisted of a circular room and a set of stairs in the middle leading up to the top level where the lookout station was located.

"Wait," he said, remembering. "There's a set of walkie-talkies and binoculars on the top level."

Charlotte clicked on the flashlight and started for the stairs. He went after her and they climbed until they reached the lookout area.

"Over there." Jonas spotted the walkie-talkies

the rangers used to communicate during fires. "There's the binoculars."

Charlotte grabbed the walkie-talkie. "This is Deputy Charlotte Walker. Is anyone within range?" She tried several channels without an answer. "We're not close enough to a receiver. Can you see anything through the binoculars?"

He focused below. "Nothing but darkness."

She blew out a sigh. "We'll take the walkie talkies with us and the binoculars. Once this is over, we'll return them to the station."

While it was nice to be out of the dampness and cold, staying in one place for long was a bad idea. Jonas slowly descended the steps with Charlotte right behind him.

On the ground floor, Annie stood alert near the door.

Charlotte went over to the closet and opened it. "There's bottled water." She handed him a water and took one for herself and gave some to the dog. "There are some heavy fireproof jackets inside. They'll keep us warmer."

He drank deep. "I'll take the warmth over the weight any day."

She smiled up at him and slipped on one of the jackets and gave him the other.

Jonas shrugged into the jacket. "Let's get out of here." Jonas slung the binoculars strap around his neck and took up walking in the direction they'd been heading.

Charlotte tried the walkie-talkie once more and shook her head before sticking it into her pocket. "Hopefully we'll get into range soon enough."

Though still some distance from the base of the Root Mountains, the ground beneath their feet had been steadily climbing.

Jonas's skin crawled—he felt as if danger could be coming at them from any direction.

"So, you still enjoy trapping in the mountains?" Charlotte asked him.

"I wasn't so sure I would anymore. Last winter was the first time since..." He hadn't been able to do much trapping before because everywhere he looked, his mistakes taunted him.

"I know what you mean. I haven't been up to the mountain where Ryan fell since his death." She chanced a look his way. "We used to love hiking that mountain. We did it so many times but since then..."

He of all people understood. "It's hard. People expect you to move on and I suppose it's the right thing to do, but it's still hard."

"Yes. My friends have all tried to fix me up with someone new, but I can't." She shook her head.

For some reason, the fact her friends wanted

to set Charlotte up didn't sit well with him, but Jonas decided to let it go.

"Did you hear something?" Charlotte asked and he focused on their surroundings.

"No, nothing."

She shook her head. "Perhaps I'm being paranoid, but I thought I heard something."

"It could be an animal, but to be safe, let's keep moving." The tension in his stomach churned out acid when Annie suddenly stopped, the hair on her back raising. The dog let out a low growl.

"What is it?" Charlotte barely got the words out before the woods around them moved. The dog charged forward. A half dozen men stepped from the trees.

NINE

"No, Annie, stop." Charlotte called out to her partner when one of the men aimed his weapon at the charging animal.

Annie halted abruptly. The man lowered his weapon. With an order from someone in charge, the soldiers advanced on them with precision. None appeared concerned about her K-9 partner, but they didn't know Annie. She was a warrior and zealous when it came to defending Charlotte.

"Drop your weapons." The order came from the same person. A tanned man dressed entirely in black wore a knit cap pulled down low. The look on his face was like looking into darkness itself.

The ones surrounding them halted a few feet away, with their weapons trained on Charlotte and Jonas.

Annie moved to Charlotte's side unopposed.

Charlotte's heart sank. This was all on her. She should have gone with Lainey and Abram to the station. If she had, there would be a team to back her up before heading to Harley's. Instead, her actions had led to her and Jonas's capture.

Jonas kept the handgun leveled at the one calling the shots while he glanced her way.

"You'd be foolish to try. Drop it." The man calling out the orders stepped closer to Jonas.

Charlotte slowly lowered her weapon to the ground. "Do as he says. They'll kill us otherwise." While she prayed that wouldn't happen if they surrendered, she and Jonas posed a threat to their illegal operation. They were better off dead.

Jonas slowly lowered his weapon to the ground.

"Get them." The leader ordered one of his people to confiscate their weapons.

The subordinate kept his attention trained on Charlotte and Jonas as he advanced. He grabbed the weapons and retreated to his position.

"Search them. There could be other weapons," the man in charge ordered.

A thorough check gave up the walkie-talkie from Charlotte's pocket. The binoculars were ripped from Jonas's neck.

Once he was certain they were no longer a threat, the boss stepped to within a few inches of them. "Where are they?"

Charlotte recoiled from the anger on his face. "I don't know what you're talking about."

"The girl and the Amish man. They escaped. Where are they?"

Charlotte shot Jonas a look. Abram and Lainey had been captured but managed to get away. If they'd been forced to hide out to avoid being caught, it would explain the delay in them reaching the sheriff.

"I have no idea where they are," Charlotte told him while her brain struggled to come up with a way to escape their captors.

"You're lying." He turned his full attention to her. "The girl was with you—we know that much. You went to the Amish man for help. So, I'll ask you again, where would they go?"

Charlotte held his gaze and tried not to show her fear. "We split up. I have no idea where they are."

"Then you'll help us find them." He motioned to several of the men who grabbed hers and Jonas's arms. "Bring them." She and Jonas were hauled along with the group while Charlotte gave the hand signal to Annie to fall back. She wouldn't put it past these creeps to shoot her partner.

Annie fell back and trotted into the woods while garnering only a passing notice from a few of their captors. Annie would keep following. The first opportunity she got she'd come to Charlotte's aide.

They were heading to the camp. With her and Jonas in custody, there were only two people standing in the way of the crimes committed here being buried forever. She and Jonas didn't have much time to figure out a way to escape.

Charlotte caught Jonas's attention. *We have to escape*, she mouthed and hoped he understood enough. He slowly nodded and she whispered, "As soon as we have the chance."

After walking for some time, the camp came into view.

"Get them inside and watch them," the boss said. "I'm checking in." The leader stopped in front of the dining hall. The two men guarding her and Jonas clutched their arms and headed for it. "You two—go with them."

Charlotte's heart sank. There would be four to overpower.

Inside the dining hall, she and Jonas were forced into chairs.

"Don't try anything," one of their guards barked at them.

The four stepped a little away. Charlotte couldn't believe those men hadn't tied them up. She watched as they walked around the dining room. Most appeared on edge. She leaned over closer to Jonas. "This is our only chance. We won't have long. I have no doubt they'll kill us soon once we can't help them find Lainey and Abram."

"What do you want to do?"

"I'm going to fake becoming ill. When I fall on the floor, call them over. Do whatever is necessary to overpower them quickly."

He swallowed deeply and held her gaze. Both recognized the impossible odds they faced.

Charlotte closed her eyes. *Give us strength, Lord. We need Your help.*

Though she'd grown up in a Christian home and was a Christian, Ryan's passing had shaken her faith. She'd stopped talking to God. If she were being honest, she blamed Him as well as herself for Ryan's death. Now, when she was at the end of her strength, Charlotte realized she and Jonas needed God's help to live.

As soon as the final amen slipped through her head, she went into action and shoved the chair back before dropping to the floor writhing around.

"Help, there's something wrong with her," Jonas called out.

All four men ran their way.

"Get up. What do you think you're doing?" one asked.

While all four looked down at her, Jonas jumped up to his feet and grabbed his chair. He swung it at the nearest man and hit him hard. He fell to the floor, knocked out. The closest man charged for Jonas who wielded the chair again.

Charlotte took advantage of the distraction and snatched the weapon of the man standing closest. She vaulted to her feet and ordered, "Get your hands in the air." Instead of obeying, he dove for her. It was going to be a fight to the end. She didn't want to fire the weapon and alert others. Instead, Charlotte slammed it into his forehead before he grabbed her. A look of surprise was almost comical before his eyes snapped shut and he dropped to the floor near his partner.

"Put it down," the third guard demanded with his gun aimed at Charlotte's head.

"I'm not going to do that." Charlotte was surprised at the steadiness in her voice as she trained her weapon on him.

A crashing sound jerked her opponent's attention away. Jonas was struggling with the second conscious man. It was all she needed to quickly slam the butt of the handgun against his head. With her guy incapacitated, she rushed to assist Jonas.

He was pinned against the table. Charlotte grabbed the perp and pulled him off. Before she could get the weapon into position to threaten, the man whirled and slammed his fist against her jaw, sending her flying backward. Her attacker reached her in two quick steps and grabbed her throat. Desperate, Charlotte's frightened gaze spotted Jonas once more with the chair. *Hold on*, she told herself and tried not to panic.

The chair smashed against the man's back. He fell forward and the weight of the unconscious man drove her to the floor.

Charlotte scrambled out from under him with Jonas's help.

"Check for weapons and phones," she told him and felt inside her perp's pockets. He had a weapon but no phone. After a thorough exam, they had four additional weapons and clips but no cells, which meant no means to communicate with her people, and Charlotte had no idea where Lainey and Abram were.

"Let's get out of here. I don't see how others didn't hear the commotion." Charlotte ran to the rear exit and slowly opened the door. Jonas slipped out behind her. The woods were just a short distance from the back of the dining room.

"Run and don't stop," she told him. "We don't have long before they come after us." They fled.

Annie appeared in the woods in front of them. Charlotte and Jonas reached the trees and kept going.

"We need to get back on track with finding the women, but I'm scared for Lainey and Abram." Charlotte held the denim jacket out to Annie. Her partner detected the trace scent left behind by its owner and veered to the left. Charlotte and Jonas ran after the dog, happy to get as far away from their attackers as possible.

They kept pace with Annie until they'd put a significant amount of space between themselves and the camp. "I believe we can slow down now," Charlotte said. "As happy as I am that Abram and Lainey were able to escape their captors, if they're still in the woods, both are in danger. You've seen the amount of people searching for us." She hated to consider how frightened Lainey must be.

"Abram knows this countryside well," Jonas reminded her. "He will keep them hidden."

Charlotte smiled. She would have to trust Abram to keep them safe, but one thing was glaringly clear. "There's no one coming to help us, Jonas. We're on our own." She looked behind them. Not a single light showed.

His attention went to the dog. "You said Annie's collar has a GPS signal attached to it. Your people might already be tracking us."

He was trying to put a positive spin on the situation, and she was grateful. Charlotte searched his face. If she'd called for backup to search for Lainey instead of going it alone, none of this would be happening.

He must have seen the doubt in her eyes because he said, "This isn't your fault, Charlotte—

none of it. You were trying to help a friend in trouble. You saved Lainey's life."

Charlotte wished she felt the same way. "And now Lainey and Abram are both in danger like us."

He stepped closer and brushed his fingers across her cheek, sending a chill trailing after his touch. "We're still alive and fighting. After everything we've gone through, we haven't given up."

She leaned into his hand for a moment. Was it just the circumstances that had thrown them together that was responsible for the way she felt when she looked into his eyes? Honestly, Charlotte barely knew him...except that he was strong and courageous and hadn't left her side despite facing down death multiple times.

This isn't real...

It couldn't be. Because if she were capable of feeling something for Jonas, it meant she'd begun letting go of Ryan and she wasn't ready.

Charlotte reached up and clasped Jonas's hand for a second before letting him go.

"Then it's settled," she said in a breathy voice. "We go after Harley and the women."

Jonas slowly agreed. "We better keep moving," he said in a voice as unsteady as hers. "Annie's getting ahead and there could be more out here looking for us."

She shivered at the thought. It was terrifying that so many were coming after them. How big was this operation and who was the person calling the shots?

For the moment, the bad guys were the last thing on his mind. Jonas kept replaying the tender moment between himself and Charlotte. For the first time since he'd lost Ivy, he had feelings for another woman and it scared him. He'd lived a life of solitude for the past six years, living in self-imposed isolation because he didn't believe himself worthy of being happy again. Yet, despite their circumstances, Charlotte made him smile whenever he glanced at her.

If he let her into his heart—if she became important to him like Ivy and their baby had—could he survive if the relationship didn't work out? His heart was so fragile now. Jonas wasn't so sure he'd recover from another loss.

"I still think we're missing something." The woman dominating his thoughts spoke, giving him the excuse he needed not to examine his heart too closely.

"Such as?" He cleared his throat to cover up the roughness that had everything to do with her.

"Like who is really in charge of this organization because it sure isn't Harley."

Jonas didn't see Harley as a leader, either.

The man had a temper and had caused plenty of scenes when things didn't go his way. And the violence he showed toward Betty spoke of someone dangerous.

"I've been thinking about the times Harley has gotten arrested and somehow gotten off. I believe the real person in charge is someone with enough power to get him out of anything."

Jonas stopped at the very idea. "Like someone in law enforcement?"

It was clear she hadn't considered the option. "Oh, no, I sure hope you're wrong. I'm friends with everyone in the sheriff's department, and each is as good as they get. I trust them," she stressed.

"What about the local police?" Jonas heard noises coming from the direction of the camp.

Charlotte froze. "They're coming. Let's go."

They hit a fast pace.

While worrying about those coming after them, Jonas thought on the little he'd heard about the local police. Most seemed nice enough. It was a small department. Was it possible someone from the force was running an illegal trafficking ring?

"Jonas, they're gaining," Charlotte whispered. "We've got to get out of sight." She looked around for someplace to hide.

Charlotte pointed to a spot that was overgrown

with brush. With Annie close, they knelt behind the camouflage, huddled close together.

After a handful of tense moments, several sets of footsteps tramped through the woods near them. Jonas clenched his hand and held his breath.

"Any sign of them?" a man whispered almost inaudibly. Jonas recognized the voice of the one calling the shots from earlier.

"Nothing yet but they can't have gotten far," another replied lowly.

"This is the last thing we need," the leader responded. "Especially with the deal almost in place."

Each man's voice was little more than a whisper. Jonas turned his head slightly, uncertain he'd heard correctly until he saw Charlotte's eyes widen. She'd been right. There was something more going on.

"Yeah, well, if this gets out, you can forget about a deal. Harley set all of this in motion," a new man Jonas didn't recognize was now speaking.

"Harley has no business being in any form of leadership and I've told Elliott this for a while. I figured it was only a matter of time before Harley screwed something up and got us all caught." This was the leader again. Jonas strained to hear him clearly. "I tell you what, if those two get to a phone and bring the sheriff's department into this, we'd better clear out quickly and get rid of our weakest link fast, as well as the girls."

No one answered that dreadful claim.

Anger rose inside Jonas.

Everyone involved would disappear into the darkness and probably set up operations in another part of the state.

Conversation ended and soon those following them were on the move. Jonas waited through a long, intense silence before he finally rose and held his hand out to Charlotte.

"It should be safe to start walking again," he told her. "The only problem is, they're heading in the same direction we need to go."

"We'll have to give them a wide berth. We can't afford to get captured again. Too much is at stake."

Jonas replayed the conversation he'd heard in his head. "Are you acquainted with someone by the name of Elliott?" He was surprised one of the men had mentioned a name.

"No…" Charlotte's hand flew to her mouth. "Wait, I am…but it can't be him. He's a police officer and a friend of mine."

Jonas's stomach plummeted. "We said the person in charge could be in law enforcement."

Charlotte clearly didn't want to consider it might be her friend. "But Elliott Shores has a wife and two little girls. It can't be him." Her troubled eyes searched his face hoping he would deny it. For her sake, Jonas hoped he was wrong.

Once more he thought about all the different vehicles he'd seen traveling down his dirt road toward Harley's. Most of the time it was at night. Occasionally during the day.

Jonas recalled one time in particular. He'd stepped out on his porch. A car he didn't know passed by his place just as it was getting dark. There were four men inside. He hadn't recognized any of them.

"I really hope this isn't Elliott, but he was acquainted with Ryan and we can't afford to rule him out at this point. Elliott works in the department's human trafficking task force."

The irony of the statement was not lost on Jonas. "If this is him, then he'd have access to what groups the police are targeting, and he'd understand how to avoid the area where other suspected rings operate."

Charlotte clearly wasn't ready to accept that her friend might be the enemy. "Elliott is more of the type to take orders than give them, although he'd kill me for saying as much." She seemed to realize what she'd said and clamped her hand over her mouth again.

"I guess it's possible there's another side to him you haven't seen," Jonas said gently. "If he's involved in trafficking and has the gall to work on the police department's task force to bring down human trafficking rings, then he's obviously not the person you thought you knew."

She shuddered. "You're right."

Annie kept her nose to the ground, sniffing out the scent belonging to the young woman who possessed the denim jacket.

If this Elliott Shores was involved, perhaps he wasn't the one in charge and just another person in a large organization.

"If he is involved, it's a frightening thought." Charlotte sighed. "How many others in law enforcement are working for this organization?"

The world in which these things took place was one he couldn't imagine. "There are times like this when I miss being Amish," he told her honestly. "They are far from perfect, but it seems like the *Englischer* world is so far removed from those simple ways."

"You're right—it is. Do you think you'd ever return to the faith?" she asked, her attention on his face.

He answered the question honestly. "I am no longer the same person."

"But you still live their way for the most part. You don't own a car or a phone."

He could tell she thought this odd. "I guess it's hard to completely let go of the only way of life

I've ever known. I am content with my life as it is." Was he? He had been simply existing for so long. Hiding out on his little piece of property and holding vigil to his dead wife.

Jonas had lost track of how long they'd been on the run. The long time spent moving without rest were taking their toll. He tried to figure out how many hours had passed and couldn't. A guess would be they'd started a new day by now, which meant they may have hours still of walking in the dark before the sun would guide them.

The sudden sound of voices speaking loudly, without trying to disguise their presence, was so strange that it took him a second to figure out it was real.

He and Charlotte found a safe place to hide and headed for it. She gave a hand signal for the dog to follow.

"Where's it coming from?" he whispered close to her ear. The fog that continued to make life miserable also made determining the location of the sounds hard. When she didn't answer, he turned his head her way. "Charlotte?"

Her huge green eyes found him. "It's coming from straight ahead and I recognize one of the voices. It's Elliott Shores." A dirty cop.

TEN

"Let's get out of here. Now." Yet before Charlotte had taken a single step, a snatch of conversation stopped her in her tracks. She grabbed Jonas's arm, keeping him there.

The disbelief on Jonas's face confirmed he'd also heard what was said. "They have Lainey and Abram…"

"I want to get closer to see if we can figure out where they're being held," Charlotte said. "We stand a chance at rescuing them."

Jonas immediately shook his head. "Not a good idea."

"We have to try." Charlotte signaled for Annie to stay while she carefully moved forward one tree at a time, Jonas trailing her, until they were close enough to hear the conversation clearly.

"They're holding the girl and that Amish man at the abandoned Christian camp," Elliott was saying, "I want to speak to them further and see who else they've told about us."

"What about the other two? One's a cop. Shouldn't we be focused on them?" The man in the knit cap who was giving orders before didn't seem to like the change in plans.

"They're not going anywhere," Elliot said. "We have men stationed in the woods and on all the roads leading to town, and there's no houses around for them to call for help." Elliott's annoyed-sounding sigh reached her. Charlotte went emotionally numb. Someone she called a friend was involved in this terrible operation.

"We have far more pressing things to deal with. Harley needs to be found and dealt with," Elliott announced to his people.

They wanted Harley dead.

"You want us to take care of the matter while you take some men and speak to the two at the camp?" the leader from before said without any hint of remorse.

"That's not our place. We'll let him take care of Harley."

Charlotte's attention pivoted to Jonas. Elliott just confirmed he wasn't the one in calling the shots. There was someone bigger heading this up.

Multiple footsteps started toward them.

Charlotte ducked out of sight along with Jonas. Flashlights panned all around while she held her breath and prayed Elliott's people hadn't heard the movement.

While they hunkered down, the number of people with Elliott kept coming. She counted almost a dozen. After the last person passed by, Charlotte let go of her breath. At least they weren't spotted.

Lainey and Abram needed help. Once Elliott's people figured out the two didn't know anything, they'd be dead.

Lord, please keep those young women safe until we can help them.

"Let's give them time to get ahead of us before we follow," Jonas whispered, coming to the same conclusion as Charlotte.

Seconds ticked by. "It should be safe to leave," Charlotte said and called Annie to her side. Keeping her attention on those ahead, a dreadful thought turned Charlotte's stomach. "What if Elliott was the one who ordered Ryan's death? Or worse, what if he killed Ryan and Michaela?" The thought of Ryan being betrayed by someone Charlotte called a friend sickened her. She remembered all the time she and Elliott had discussed what happened. Elliott was a witness to how devastated she was by losing Ryan. He'd been a huge support. Was it all an act?

"We don't know anything for certain yet."

She forced herself to let go of the betrayal she felt toward Elliott. She had a job to do. "I pray Lainey's grandmother decided to call the sheriff's office instead of waiting. If she did, Sheriff McCallister will realize I have Annie with me, and he'll check her GPS."

But she couldn't count on this happening in time to save Lainey and Abram. "I hope she did. There are so many men," Charlotte said. "Our only chance to save Abram and Lainey is to get in and out without the bad guys figuring out we were there. Still, we can't keep wandering through the woods without eventually getting caught."

She couldn't get what Elliott had said out of her head.

"I'm sorry your friend Elliott is involved," Jonas said.

"Me, too." She gave a sad smile. "With Elliott's involvement, we must look at this entire organization differently. There could be more people in the law enforcement community involved." Knowing that someone who had sworn to protect the ones who were being trafficked was involved was a heart-wrenching thought.

Charlotte's heart broke over the decision they were now forced to make, choosing between saving the innocent girls and rescuing her friend and Abram.

"I sure hope we can find Lainey and Abram soon and save them. I have a feeling time is running out on the girls. We won't have long to reach them before they're moved. I wonder if Harley realizes his people have turned on him?"

Jonas nodded. "It would explain why no one's been able to reach him. If Harley is one small cog in this operation, would he be aware of the next step after he'd delivered the girls?"

She thought about his question. "Probably not. It sounds as if Harley is one who kidnaps the girls and from there someone else takes them to another location. From what we've overheard, Harley has been getting sloppy for some time and has become a liability. If he was the one who took Michaela and had to let her go, then I don't understand why they would trust him to keep grabbing girls."

Jonas rubbed his beard thoughtfully. "Unless Harley has something on Elliott, or the real person in charge."

Charlotte hadn't considered it before. "Harley's not above blackmail."

"No, he isn't. Using that theory, I'm wondering if perhaps he wasn't the one who killed Michaela but saw the person who did—Elliott or the one in charge. He might even have evidence against them."

Her eyes widened. "If we can get to Harley and save the women, we might be able to talk him into cooperating." Her thoughts went to Betty. "I can't imagine Betty being aware of what Harley was doing, but she might have seen something useful."

Jonas shook his head. "I guess, but in my opinion, she's another victim like those girls."

Charlotte didn't want to think about Betty paying the price for Harley's crimes with her life. "She wasn't at the house."

"He may have her with him. He may have forced her to go. If so, she's bound to have figured out what Harley's been up to by now. She could be a major witness against him if we can convince her to cooperate."

Charlotte shook her head. So many innocent people's lives were in danger all because of greed.

Since it was dark and Jonas probably hadn't seen Elliott clearly, she described him. Thin, barely five foot eight. His sandy brown hair had been receding for some time. "Was he the one with Betty when you heard her scream?"

The furrow between Jonas's brows deepened. "He doesn't sound like the same man. The person I saw had dark hair and was at least six-two or more."

She sighed. "That's not Elliott. I was hoping we could connect him to Harley and..." And what? She had no idea what Elliott being at Harley's house would prove other than they knew each other.

"It was a good thought." Jonas glanced around

at their surroundings. "We have to be getting close to the camp by now."

"I'm not sure what to do once we reach it," she admitted. "Hopefully, we can locate where they're holding Lainey and Abram and find a way to get them out."

They kept moving, Annie at their side, keeping a safe distance from Elliot and the men ahead of them. They'd been walking around in circles for hours since they'd left Abram's house and were no closer to understanding what was happening or escaping than when they'd first begun the trek to Harley's house.

Up ahead, the woods cleared. Charlotte pointed to the back of the closest building. If they could make it there, perhaps they could find a way to get close enough to figure out where Lainey and Abram were being held.

She and Jonas slipped to the back of the building and then down the side until they were near the front but still hidden.

"I don't see anything," Charlotte whispered. It stood to reason they would have moved Lainey and Abram out of sight.

"Over there." He pointed to the building where she and Jonas had been held before. "There's a bunch of soldiers near the front."

"That's it. Let's circle around behind and see

if we can get closer." They started toward the dining hall while doing their best to stay hidden.

Several times, Charlotte halted abruptly when snatches of conversation seemed to indicate the men guarding the building were on high alert.

"They're expecting us," she whispered to Jonas. "We can't get captured." They were Lainey and Abram's only hope in avoiding certain death.

Once they reached the back of the dining hall, Charlotte made sure there wasn't anyone standing guard around back. Advancing to the building, she saw that the windows were too high up to see inside without being on the porch.

She tentatively managed the first step and held her breath when a board creaked under her foot. When the people inside didn't appear to hear she climbed the rest of them until she was standing on the porch.

Jonas avoided the noisy board and traversed the stairs. Edging closer to the windows, Charlotte stood on one side while Jonas moved to the other.

The building was mostly dark. Someone had lit a couple of candles and placed them around to give light.

Charlotte searched the dining room until she spotted Lainey and Abram in the corner and pointed to their location. Both were seated at one of the tables, their arms secured behind them.

The men weren't taking any chances of them escaping like Charlotte and Jonas had.

She could see the strain on Lainey's face even from here. Charlotte couldn't imagine the pain she was suffering from the gunshot wound with her hands secured.

She looked around the room. Where were the men watching them?

While she contemplated the best course of action, several men came from the kitchen area. More candles were lit. She recognized Elliott right away and noticed something she hadn't been able to detect before. Elliott was dressed in his police uniform.

He stepped over to where Lainey and Abram were held. "So, we meet again," he said with a smirk on his face.

He'd run into them before.

"You tricked us," Lainey said as she looked at him in fear. "You let us believe you were going to help us."

Charlotte's shoulders slumped. Elliott had used his position as a police officer to lure them into believing he was one of the good guys. He and his people had probably been looking for Lainey and Abram the way they were her and Jonas. Lainey would have trusted Elliott because of the uniform.

"Yes, I did, and you believed me, so we both

messed up." Though Elliott wasn't a big man, his current position of authority over these two innocent people probably made him feel important. Charlotte did her best to control her revulsion. Her first instinct was to charge inside and confront Elliott with what she suspected. But if she did, she'd be signing all their death warrants.

He deliberately put pressure on Lainey's wound. She screamed in pain. Elliott seemed pleased. "Where are they going?" Elliott didn't waste time getting to what he wanted to know. "They were with you at one point. They sent you to get help. You have some idea what's planned."

Lainey dropped her eyes to the table without answering. Elliott's face twisted as his anger grew. He grabbed hold of Abram's head and pointed his weapon at his temple. "Speak or he dies."

"No, don't!" Lainey pleaded. "I don't have any idea where they are now. They were supposed to go to Harley's house and…"

Elliott leaned in closer, likely to intimidate. "And what?"

"And they were going to try and get Charlotte's phone back."

Elliott jerked back. After a long minute he let Abram go.

Charlotte bit her lip and prayed Elliott wouldn't realize the real reason why she and Jonas had returned to the place where she'd been taken.

"They needed a way to call for help in case we failed to reach the sheriff's department," Lainey added to make her story believable.

Elliott stared her down for a long moment. "They were at the house but got away. Where would they go from there?"

Lainey stared at him with her eyes filled with tears. "The plan was to get the phone and call for help."

Elliott shook his head. "They didn't. The phone wasn't at the house. Harley has it. So, I'll ask you again, where would they go from there?"

Lainey struggled to come up with an answer. "I don't know," she insisted again.

Her response displeased Elliott. Once more he pushed his fingers onto her gunshot. Lainey bit her bottom lip to keep from screaming again.

One thing became very clear—Elliott wasn't the smartest person. He didn't notice Lainey was making up her answers.

"All right, let's suppose you're telling the truth," he said. "You must have some idea where they'd go?"

Lainey watched him with huge fearful eyes.

When she didn't answer, Elliott stuck his face inches from hers. "Who did *you* tell about what was happening?"

"No one. You found us before we reached a phone."

"Oh, no," Charlotte whispered. If Elliott was convinced no one was coming to assist, he had no reason to keep Lainey and Abram alive.

"Good." Pleased, Elliott stepped away, and Charlotte couldn't hear what he said.

Soon, Elliott and his goons left the dining hall. This was it. She moved to Jonas's side. "We have to act now."

Jonas slipped to the back door. Opening it made only the slightest of sounds, yet both Lainey and Abram heard it.

Charlotte placed her finger to her lips before Lainey could say a word.

Once they reached the table, Jonas examined Lainey and Abram's ties. Their hands were secured behind the chair backs. "We need some way to cut their restraints."

"I have a knife inside my pocket," Abram told them. "No one searched us."

Jonas retrieved it and cut both their restraints away. "We must hurry. They'll come back soon."

Charlotte stayed close to Lainey as they covered the space to the door. Slipping outside, she ran with Lainey toward the trees where Annie waited. A heartbeat later, Jonas and Abram reached the safe spot.

"I'm so happy to see you." Lainey said through tears. "I was afraid they'd killed you."

"I'm happy you're both okay," Charlotte replied, smiling at Abram, too, "How's your shoulder?" Her mouth thinned as she recalled Elliott's actions.

"It's okay," Lainey assured her even though she appeared quite pale from the ordeal.

"We need to keep moving." Charlotte started through the trees, not sure if they were heading anywhere close to the direction of Harley's mountain house.

Jonas kept close attention behind them. "So far, I don't see anyone following yet. As soon as they realize Lainey and Abram are gone, they'll figure we're involved."

"I have something that might help." Lainey dug into her pocket and pulled out a cell phone.

"Where did you get this?" Charlotte asked, unable to accept what she was seeing.

Lainey smiled at her reaction. "One of those men left it on the counter before they tied us up. I grabbed it and stuffed it in my pocket." Charlotte didn't miss how Abram gazed at Lainey with what looked like fondness and admiration as she held the phone out to Charlotte.

"Thank you, Lainey." Charlotte accepted the phone and tried to call 9-1-1. The frustration of the call not going through was enough to double her over. "There's no service here. Let's keep going. Hopefully, we can pick up some along the way."

Flashlights pierced the darkness behind them. "Someone's coming. They'll spread out and search every square inch of this place." Jonas's words reinforced the urgency.

"He's right." Charlotte slipped the cell phone into her pocket and grabbed hold of Lainey's arm once more. Together with Jonas and Abram they ran.

At this point, they were simply trying to survive. She'd figure out the best way to get to the girls after they were safe. For the moment, saving the lives of those with her was the most important thing. Because if they died, the secrets that Elliott and Harley were willing to kill to cover up would die with them.

Jonas studied the lights. "They're going in a different direction. At least that's something. Still, we have no idea how many others are out there and have been alerted to our escape. We need help." And he had no idea how to get it for them.

"Give us a minute," Charlotte told Lainey and Abram. "Annie, stay." She reached for Jonas's arm and tugged him out of earshot. Both Lainey and Abram huddled together, their troubled gazes darting around the darkness.

She tried the cell phone once more before shaking her head. "I'm still not picking up any service. What do you suggest?"

Jonas kept his fading hope to himself. It seemed everything they tried ended badly. He ran his hand through his damp hair and struggled to come up with a plan to get them out of this mess. To pick up service, they'd need to get out of the trees. He could think of only one way. "What about the fire tower from earlier? I don't believe it's that far from here. The service should be better."

Relief flashed across Charlotte's face. "You're right. It's perfect." Her smile disappeared just as quickly. "Jonas, those girls. They're in danger every second Harley has them."

"We have no choice. We can't let them die."

She shook her head. "You should stay with Lainey and Abram. Get to the tower and call for help."

He stepped closer. "I'm not letting you go after Harley alone. We have no idea what kind of state he's in or if there are others with him." And he cared too much about her to let her go it alone.

She didn't look away, and for a long moment their fears slipped into the background and it was just her and him, and he had hope again. Despite facing death and not being sure they were going to make it out of this thing alive, he had hope.

"I don't think it's a good idea for Lainey and Abram to go on alone," she said, breaking the moment.

Jonas held her gaze. "If we want to try and save those girls, I don't think we have a choice. The stakes are higher now. Those men have a deal to make and will try to wrap it up quickly because they think the sheriff has been called. Elliott will contact the people watching the girls soon enough and have them moved. This might be our only chance to rescue them."

She glanced over to where Abram and Lainey stood, obviously trying to make the right decision. He knew she didn't want to make a mistake. "Okay," she said finally. "Do you think Abram will be able to find the tower with Lainey?"

Jonas had no doubt. "Abram is a *gut* hunter. He will be able to locate it. It's best if they stay there at the tower. They'll be out of the elements, and it will make it easier for the sheriff's people to find them. They should be safe enough." Unless Elliott and his people searched the tower.

It wasn't necessary to say the words out loud. Charlotte understood the risks.

"We'd better hurry," she said, breaking the silence he was happy to let go on forever. Here in the small space between them existed nothing dangerous or evil.

But the people coming after them needed to silence them. Even though they didn't fully grasp the truth of how far-reaching this operation was, what he and Charlotte had seen was enough to put people away.

He reluctantly stepped back. Together they told Lainey and Abram the plan.

"What if we're caught?" Lainey asked anxiously. "I'm afraid."

Charlotte reached for her hand. "You'll be okay. Abram will be with you."

Abram nodded. "I'm familiar with where the tower is. I'll get us there safely. And Charlotte is right. We should be secure there."

Jonas prayed that would prove to be the truth.

Charlotte handed the cell phone back to Lainey. "We are counting on you and Abram to reach the tower and call for help."

Lainey slowly accepted it.

"Good," Charlotte said. "Keep trying 9-1-1 along the way, and once you get service, tell them what happened."

"But where will you be?" Lainey asked.

"We're going to try and save the rest of the girls." She turned to Lainey. "Can you tell them we're heading to Harley Owens's house in the mountains so the sheriff and his people can find us?"

Lainey assured her they would.

Jonas clapped his former *bruder*-in-law's shoulder. "Be careful, Abram. If they catch any of us again, they won't hesitate to kill."

Abram's chin rose. "I will be careful. There's a lot at stake." He glanced Lainey's way, and she looked at him as Ivy had once looked at Jonas.

Was there something forming between these two or was it simply the dangerous situation they faced making Abram protective?

"Here, take this," Jonas handed his friend one of the weapons they'd taken.

Charlotte did the same to Lainey, who reluctantly took the weapon. It was a good thing they'd taken all four guns from the guards the last time they escaped capture. "Just remember what your father taught you about using a weapon."

Lainey nodded.

Abram reached for Lainey's arm and started away.

Charlotte stared after them for a moment. "I sure hope we didn't send them to their deaths."

The reality of those words had him struggling for something positive to say. "Abram is a skilled shot. Although he's Amish and a pacifist, he'll do whatever is necessary to defend Lainey and himself. We made the best decision we could to help everyone involved. We'd better get going. It's not wise to stay in one place for too long."

The flashlights had moved away from their location. If their pursuers kept going the way they were, then Abram and Lainey should be safe.

Charlotte wrapped her arms around herself to

stay warm as the cold worked its way down deep past the fireman's jacket she wore.

Jonas gathered his bearings and started walking toward the dark silhouette of the mountain that was in the distance. The biggest thought going through his head was all those innocent girls who were being held by Harley. Were they still alive?

He shared his fears with Charlotte. "Harley is all about protecting himself. He won't think twice about killing them if it means saving himself."

Charlotte was on edge like him and constantly reacting to every little sound in the woods. "This is such a terrible situation. I still can't fathom what's happening now might have ties to Ryan and Michaela's deaths."

He'd never been involved in anything as sinister as murder before. His part in Ivy's death was bad enough, but he couldn't imagine willingly taking someone's life.

Charlotte rubbed her forehead. "I believe Michaela saw something more than what she told us at the party. Whatever it was, she had to die." She stopped so suddenly it had his full attention. "Oh, no." Startled eyes found him. "I think I know what it was."

The expression on her face confirmed this was going to be bad.

ELEVEN

Why hadn't she remembered this before now? With everything that had happened following Ryan's death, she'd just completely forgot.

"What do you remember?" Jonas frowned as he waited.

"Something Michaela's mother told me after her funeral. She said her daughter was convinced someone was following her after the incident at the party. She was scared. She thought it might have something to do with her friend Sasha's disappearance. Her mother urged her to go to the police. She said Michaela planned to reach out and then she disappeared."

She recalled the conversation. "There was no report made with our people. Wyatt checked with the local police, and they hadn't received one, either."

"Unless she did call the police and somehow spoke to Elliott. I know the department has been short staffed from time to time. Elliott mentioned once he'd been forced to answer dispatch calls."

The reality of those words slapped her in the face. "Oh, no. This must be what happened. Michaela's mother was so sure her daughter had called to report what happened."

"She probably did." Jonas's mouth twisted grimly. "She never stood a chance."

Charlotte's heart broke for Michaela and her family. If only she'd reported the stalking to the sheriff's department. Or if Charlotte had followed up with Michaela about the incident at the ranch. At the time, she'd been so caught up in her own grief over losing Ryan that she hadn't been able to function for a long time. "Michaela's family was devastated by her death. They never considered she would take her own life and they did everything possible to get the coroner to change the cause of death from suicide, but he seemed certain she killed herself."

So many people found Michaela's death suspicious. The scene appeared staged, but they also trusted the system and didn't suspect that dirty cops might be involved.

"Dr. McCarthy is usually a reasonable man and he's been the county's coroner for as long as I can remember. My dad thought very highly of him."

"Has he ever been wrong about a cause of death before?"

Charlotte thought about it for a moment. "I don't believe anyone's ever disputed his ruling before." She'd tried to convince him to do additional testing on Michaela to be certain, but he'd gotten angry and told her the cause of death stood as suicide. He'd ruled Ryan's death an accident. At the time, she'd found his change in temper odd, but he'd been quick to soften toward her, saying they couldn't dispute the science. The deaths had rocked the whole community, certainly her whole world, so she'd understood if he was on edge. "Once this is over, we have to seriously look into both deaths." She paused, trying to get her next words out. "What if Dr. McCarthy's involved in what's happening?"

"Could he be the one in charge?"

"I guess." But she had doubts. "He's the coroner for the county. He might be able to fix the cause of death, but he certainly couldn't keep a human trafficking pipeline hidden from the public."

Jonas nodded. "Obviously there's at least one law enforcement officer involved—probably others. It's possible they have people in various positions of authority to keep things moving smoothly."

Charlotte combed her fingers through her tangled hair. "I believe we're beginning to see bits and pieces of a much bigger picture. I just want to find those women and get them out of there safely before it's too late. And then I want to find the people who are responsible for this and put them all in prison for a very long time. I don't think I'll ever forget this case."

Those words echoed through her head reminding her of the one case that had haunted her father during his career. A child had been taken from her home. Her dad and all the local law enforcement agencies had been called out, but the child was never recovered. Her father had kept a photo of the little girl in his wallet. Through the years until he retired, every chance he got he'd go over her file searching for something he might have missed.

There were cases that haunted a person long after they ended. Michaela's case was like that for Charlotte. She hadn't been able to let it go despite the coroner's ruling. She'd gone over every single piece of evidence, every moment of the time on the mountain, and though she hadn't been able to see it, there was something far more sinister involved than an accidental fall and a suicide.

"I can barely stand up anymore. My legs are like jelly," Charlotte said. "Do you think we can stop for a second? I realize time is critical, but we're not going to be any good to anyone if we don't have the strength to save them."

Like him, the hours of walking, the close calls with the enemy, were taking their toll.

"Yes, that's a good idea. I'm struggling as well." Jonas found a place to sit, and he and Charlotte took a break while Annie sniffed around the ground.

In the rush to escape, they were off target. The path Harley used to travel through the woods was more to their left. After resting, he'd get Annie back on the scent.

Right now, Jonas's brain felt like it was covered in the same fog surrounding them. Thinking clearly was nearly impossible. When the previous day had started, his only concern was getting the fence finished and the cows moved. He had no idea the danger that was about to overtake those plans.

The pit that continued to grow in Jonas's stomach warned him bad people and things were closing in on them and the missing women. "Lainey didn't have any idea how many women were in the basement with her, right?" He and Charlotte could be searching for one, two, or half a dozen or more.

"No." Charlotte shifted toward him with regret on her pretty face.

He wouldn't let her apologize for what wasn't her fault. "I'd do it all over again," he said quietly. "When I saw Harley driving your vehicle, I realized you were in danger, and I couldn't stand by and do nothing."

She reached for his hand and held it between hers. "I'm glad you did. If you hadn't, both me and Lainey would be dead, and this whole thing would be swept under the rug." Her expression held admiration. "I owe you my life."

He swallowed deeply, wishing he felt deserving of her faith in him. By his carelessness, Ivy and his child had died. Helping Charlotte had made him somewhat more redeemed.

As he looked into Charlotte's face, he wondered if she hadn't saved *him* in some way. His feelings for Charlotte were changing and his guilt growing. Every time he thought about the way Ivy had loved him unconditionally, this—whatever it was happening between him and Charlotte—felt wrong. Ivy had taken Jonas how he was and hadn't tried to tame his adventurous nature. She'd encouraged him to go trapping when he should have stayed with her. Ivy had deserved a better husband than him. Finding happiness—having a future beyond Ivy—didn't seem right.

Jonas slowly pulled his hand free and rose. "We still have a long way to go, and the countryside will be rough."

After an awkward moment, Charlotte stood as well.

Jonas dusted himself off and started walking. "If we head to the left, we should intersect with the path Harley used to climb the mountain," he said without looking at her.

He knew he'd hurt her by his abrupt change. Another thing to regret. Jonas did his best to shake off the guilt.

By his calculations, they were getting close to daybreak, which meant they'd be arriving at the house where Harley hopefully had the girls around sunrise. It would be better to see in the mountainous terrain, but also dangerous should anyone follow them up the mountain.

"Look, there are tire tracks. We're back on Harley's trail."

Charlotte held the denim jacket out to Annie. The tracks had the dog's attention right away. Once she had the smell of their anonymous woman, she frantically sniffed the air until getting on the scent. When the dog was on track, she was hard to keep up with. Both Jonas and Charlotte raced to stay with her.

"I don't suppose there's a way to slip up on the house without being spotted?" Charlotte asked.

Jonas tried to recall. "I have only been by the house a couple of times and each one I had no idea anyone lived there... I'm not sure if Harley even owns it. He could have just claimed to. I wouldn't put it past him to not tell the truth."

Charlotte watched Annie work the path in front of them. "We can't let him see we're coming."

Jonas didn't respond. His thoughts kept returning to the tender moment he'd almost shared with Charlotte. Until now, he'd been content with his life. His farm was his world. Though he still prayed from time to time, his faith since losing Ivy and his child wasn't strong. It felt as if he were going through the motions most times during the silent prayers over meals. Reading his Bible was a chore that he sometimes found an excuse to skip. He'd been angry with *Gott* for letting Ivy and the baby die. Now, in the middle of a life and death situation, where more than his life was on the line, he found himself asking *Gott* to help them. He didn't want to make another mistake that would cost lives.

"Jonas?"

He jerked his head toward Charlotte and realized she'd stopped walking. "What's wrong?" Immediately he could tell something was.

She pointed to their right. "Someone's coming."

A single flashlight moved through the woods. These couldn't be the same people who had been at the camp. Whoever it was, they were coming from the wrong direction.

"Hurry, let's get out of sight." He instinctively reached for Charlotte's hand, and together they searched for a place to get out of the path of those moving their way. She called the dog off the track and Annie followed them to their hideout.

Huddled together with Annie, Jonas could almost sense Charlotte's anxiety matching his.

Soon, it became apparent there was more than one person moving through the underbrush. His heart sank. The noise was magnified. It sounded like a dozen or more people, but it was probably only a handful.

"Do we even have an idea where we're going?" one person spoke with obvious agitation.

"Keep quiet!" another snapped. "They could be close. And if we can't find them before they reach the police, it doesn't matter where we're at. It's all over for us."

The first man clearly wasn't going to be quiet. "Wasn't that supposed to be Elliot's job? To keep this off the police's radar? How did the deputy get involved, anyway?"

The group sounded as if they were right on top of Jonas and Charlotte's location.

"Look." The second man had had enough of the complainer. "None of this is Elliott's fault. He tried to fix what Harley messed up. Besides, D.A. is the one who messed up by not getting control over Harley long ago. The guy is a loose cannon and has been for a while."

D.A.? Jonas looked to Charlotte to see if she

recognized the name, but she appeared as confused as he was.

"So, keep your mouth shut and do your job if you don't want to end up in the same predicament as Harley. Understood?"

The first man snorted a response Jonas didn't hear and followed after the others. The sound of tromping through the woods echoed all around them, and Jonas had to wonder how much longer he and Charlotte would be able to stay hidden from so many who were determined they weren't going to walk out of the woods alive.

For a long time after the group had left the area, Jonas remained still, kneeling beside Charlotte.

"This just keeps getting more confusing," he said as he rose and took Charlotte's hand. "Do you recognize the initials D.A.?"

She shook her head. "No, I have no idea who they were talking about."

"You have to wonder how many people are involved in this."

Charlotte gathered her heavy jacket closer. "I'm worried. There are so many. While I'm sure we've run into several of the same people, even so, that's a lot of armed soldiers looking for us. They can't afford to let us live. Especially since there's at least one police officer involved in the trafficking ring and possibly the county coroner."

In other words, even if they were able to escape, there were some powerful people who would do their best to cover up everything, and it would be his and Charlotte's word against theirs.

Jonas tried not to lose hope, yet he wondered if, when they reached the house Harley had claimed was his, they would be walking into a trap they wouldn't be able to escape.

As they reached the mountains' foothills, the trees thinned. At the higher altitude the mountains rose above the tree line, nothing more than dark silhouettes against the night sky.

"I realize it's more dangerous for us in the daylight," Charlotte said unsteadily, "but I'm so tired of walking around in the dark."

Jonas smiled as she voiced his sentiments. "Yeah, me, too." At one time following Ivy's death, he'd practically lived in the darkness. Sleep alluded him. He'd spend hours riding or walking his property in search of some relief from his guilt. Slowly, his time in the darkness had ended. Sleep returned and yet the reprieve from the guilt remained with him still.

"You sure you can find Harley's house again in this weather?" Charlotte squinted through the fog that hung all around them.

He shoved aside the things that couldn't be changed. The life he'd imagined living—the family he and Ivy had planned for—was gone, as was the man who'd envisioned it. This shell of the person left in the wake of losing her was all he had left.

"*Jah*—yes, I believe so." He didn't tell her the many times he'd walked to the mountain and to his trapping cabin.

"How are you holding up?" Charlotte asked. Maybe she'd picked up on the strain in his voice.

"I'm fine. Just mulling everything over, I guess."

"Do you believe they made it to the tower… that they're still alive?" Charlotte asked, and he realized who she was talking about. Abram and Lainey.

"I hope so."

Charlotte looked over her shoulder once more. Both she and Jonas were on edge. "I wonder if Harley realizes they're going to kill him. After all, this was all his fault. By taking Lainey, he brought me to his door."

She was right.

"From what it sounded like," she continued, "they don't have a clue where Harley is. They're looking for him and the girls. That might work in our favor. I just hope this D.A. person doesn't have an inkling about Harley's other house." If D.A. was the actual man in charge, once he found Harley's hideout, he'd kill him and the girls, and they'd move their operation to another location. Hopefully they could get there before any of that happened.

"Me, too." Jonas hoped Harley had taken the

girls to the place in the mountains. Because if not, then he had no idea where Harley would go next, and they'd risked their lives and probably Lainey's and Abram's for nothing.

Jonas was familiar with the rugged landscape surrounding the mountains. It would take the dog miles to reach an *Englischer* home with a phone. They'd made the right call sending Lainey and Abram to the fire tower with the cell.

"I sure hope Abram and Lainey were able to reach help." Charlotte stared after Annie. She'd said as much earlier, and yet perhaps repeating that thought gave her comfort. "Because otherwise, it's just us and we're extremely outnumbered."

It wasn't the first time they'd voiced that fear tonight. And yet, those words settled around him like a bad feeling. Two or even four against so many left them at a severe disadvantage, and he wasn't sure he could protect Charlotte. He didn't want Charlotte and Abram and Lainey to sacrifice their lives. He didn't want to die and let these terrible people win. There were more lives at stake than just theirs. Many more. They might not be able to save all the women out there who were already entangled in sex trafficking, but he wanted to try to help those who'd been held with Lainey. Because they didn't deserve the nightmare coming their way.

TWELVE

Annie loped out in front of them once more as they continued walking. Charlotte noticed something she hadn't before. "She's limping. Annie, stop."

The dog immediately obeyed her request. Charlotte moved over to the dog and lifted her leg. Annie whined and Charlotte noticed what was wrong. The dog had a cut on her right front paw.

"We need to wrap the paw to limit the damage." Jonas took out his knife and cut away some of his jacket's lining.

"It's okay, Annie." Charlotte held the dog's paw while Jonas wrapped the injury gently.

"That should keep it from hurting as much." He gave Annie a pat and the dog licked his hand in appreciation.

Charlotte chuckled at Annie's response. "Thank you, Jonas, and Annie thanks you. I wonder what happened?"

"There are all sorts of dangers in the woods. It looks as if she stepped on a sharp rock."

Annie still had a slight limp as she walked but she was able to put pressure on the injured paw.

"I guess none of us are going to get through this unscathed." Charlotte pushed her hair from her face. This night had been a roller coaster ride—one innocent people had been forced upon. Yet through it all, Jonas had been there for her. He'd risked his life so many times, starting with diving into the river to pull her and Lainey from her Jeep. And she couldn't deny that his tender ministrations with her dog melted her heart a bit.

She snuck a look his way. Such a strong profile. He was a good man and yet he blamed himself for his wife's death.

Charlotte of all people understood the devastating effects the blame game could have on a person. She'd blamed herself for Ryan's death. Had allowed herself to be frozen in a moment in time and hadn't really been living at all. When she looked at Jonas, she saw something—felt something—that made her want to try, and yet how could she? Ryan was the love of her life. How could she simply move on as if his life and love meant nothing?

She couldn't. Ryan had to mean more to her than that. Time to keep moving.

Before she had the chance to take another step,

Annie growled low, the hair down her back standing at attention.

"She senses something." Dread slithered into the pit of Charlotte's stomach. She heard a sound. She'd been so wrapped up in her own thoughts she must have missed it earlier. She spun around trying to determine the direction of the noise.

"It's straight ahead," Jonas whispered. He touched her arm and motioned toward the closest coverage while Annie continued to growl and stare ahead of them.

"Annie, come." Charlotte tried to be as quiet as possible. The dog followed them over to the trees.

While they huddled together, Charlotte continued to try to place where they'd heard the noise.

"Drop your weapons and get your hands in the air—both of you," came a voice.

The bottom dropped out of Charlotte's stomach. Three armed men drew down on them.

"I said Drop. Your. Weapons."

No matter what, they couldn't surrender their weapons. Their survival was at stake.

"Now!" said the same man, with growing irritation in his tone.

Charlotte held Jonas's gaze and shook her head, praying he understood. Taking down three armed men wouldn't be easy to do, so she'd have to enlist Annie's help.

"Annie, attack." The command barely cleared

her lips before Annie charged. The lead gunman tried to fire on the dog.

Charlotte leaped to her feet and threw her weight at him before the shot could hit her partner. He stumbled backward, Annie latching on to his leg. While he screamed in pain, Charlotte wrestled the weapon from the attacker's hand and knocked him unconscious.

Immediately, another man came after Charlotte. When he spotted Annie's bared teeth, he ran. Annie flew through the air, chomping down on his arm and sending him sprawling across the ground. His weapon was shaken free.

While the man tried to push Annie off, Charlotte pinned him down with her weight. "Stop right there. Don't even think about moving." Out of the corner of her eye, she noticed Jonas disarming the final perp.

"We need to secure them to a tree," she said while giving Annie the order to release but remain close.

Jonas ripped off pieces of the inside of his jacket and tied up the man he'd taken down.

"You two are dead!" the guy yelled at him. Jonas ignored him and tore off more strips of cloth. He placed one over the man's mouth to keep him quiet. Charlotte hauled the man she was guarding over to the same tree. With Jonas's help, he was secured without incident.

He pulled at his restraints. "You'll never get out of here alive."

Charlotte stopped what she was doing as a smirk played across his face. She searched his pockets and found a cell phone.

Thank You, God.

The man's smile spread. "You have no idea who you're dealing with. This is so much bigger than anything you can imagine."

Charlotte recoiled at the confirmation of what she and Jonas suspected. "Who are you talking about? Tell us what's going on and we might be able to work out a deal on your behalf."

He laughed in her face. "I won't need a deal, and you can't even save yourselves, much less me."

Charlotte pocketed the phone and found an extra magazine for the weapon in the man's other pocket. "Last chance. Tell us about the organization, and we'll do what we can to help."

She held a strip of cloth in her hand, ready to shut him up if he didn't say what she needed to hear.

"I've got nothing to worry about," he said nonchalantly. "Do what you must. You're no threat to us. We'll still be operating long after you two are gone. It's only a matter of time before you're as dead as your boyfriend."

* * *

Jonas's eyes shot to Charlotte. All the color had left her face at that obvious taunt about Ryan.

She stepped inches from his face. "What did you say?"

The man must've realized he'd gotten under her skin because he appeared pleased. They wouldn't be getting anything useful out of him.

Jonas tugged Charlotte back, took the gag from her and secured the jeerer.

While Charlotte couldn't seem to take her eyes off the man, Jonas worked fast to get the final person tied up. He checked pockets without finding another phone. Jonas gathered all the weapons before he returned to Charlotte.

"We have to go." When she didn't move, he clasped her arm and tugged her along with him, giving Annie the command to follow.

"I'm okay," Charlotte said and snapped out of it. "He was talking about Ryan." She sounded stunned. "He all but confirmed Ryan was murdered."

"He did. This is bad on so many levels." A rush of shock raced through his body. Jonas couldn't believe what the man had said.

Charlotte drew in a breath, clearly gathering herself. "We'll get them, and we'll find out who is really in charge, but right now, we can't take a chance Abram and Lainey weren't able to call the sheriff." She brought out the criminal's phone. "It doesn't look as if the phone has been used in a while." She punched in some digits and waited. "I guess I understand why. The service is still sketchy. It could appear once we reach a higher altitude." She hung up and stuffed the phone in her pocket.

"Let's hope." Jonas thought about what the one man had said. "He sure didn't seem too worried about going to jail, even after pretty much admitting Ryan's death wasn't an accident."

Charlotte's mouth hardened. "Almost as if he thought he had a get-out-of-jail-free card."

Jonas tilted his head. "I don't understand."

"It means you don't have to worry about going to jail. It was part of a game called Monopoly. If you had a get-out-of-jail card, you didn't have to worry about going to jail." She looked back in the direction they'd come. "I'm guessing because there are law enforcement officers on his team who will protect him."

"I guess." Jonas believed it went much deeper. "But there's more to this. There must be."

She sighed and watched Annie weave her away along while on the scent. "You're right. I just wish I could figure out the identity of the real person in charge."

"Me, too. Right now, let's keep going. Once

we're above the tree line we should be able to pick up service."

He hoped it proved true.

The path continued to rise beneath their feet. The Root Mountains were not all that tall but the weather conditions at the higher altitude were always tricky.

"It feels like it's getting colder," Charlotte said and wrapped her jacket tighter.

"It probably is." He kept going over what the man had said. Was it possible that Elliott had promised those who worked for him safety from prosecution? "This Elliott person isn't very high up in his department?" he asked because he wanted to understand.

"No, he's just a patrol officer."

"So, he would only have so much power." He rubbed a hand over his tired eyes. "Who would he report to?"

Charlotte told him there was a chief of police over the officers. "I'm friends with the chief of police and he wouldn't be involved in such… Then again, I thought the same thing about Elliott. But Chief Harris is a grandfather with three girls of his own and two granddaughters. How could he turn a blind eye to what those women will be facing and still care about his own girls?" She shook her head. "But then, Elliott is married with a couple of young children himself."

"I don't understand any of this. These men are selling women for money." He knew his disgust showed in his voice. "How can anyone with a heart treat another human being in such a way?"

"It's about greed. They might not have meant for it to go this far, or for them to get in so deep. It probably started with taking a bribe to look the other way. And then before long, they were too deep to get out." She pulled in a breath. "These organizations are sometimes connected to other illegal organizations. This one could have originated in another country even."

The ways of the *Englischers* still eluded him, and he was okay with that.

"I'm going to try to call out again." She pulled out the phone and redialed.

Jonas went over to check Annie's bandage. She'd been a fierce protector and had helped save them. He lifted the dog's injured paw. The bandage was still securely in place, but it was dotted with blood. He gently placed the limb on the ground and stroked the dog's head. "You're a trooper, Annie. Hang in there."

The dog gave a low whimper in answer.

"Hello?"

Jonas's attention returned to Charlotte. The call had gone through? He hurried to her side.

"Hello, dispatch, can you hear me?" Her wide eyes found his, and she shook her head in frustration. "There's so much static." She punched end and tried again. "Hello, this is Deputy Charlotte Walker." She succinctly explained what was going on and where she and Jonas were heading. "We need immediate help. We have two civilians in the fire tower east of the Christian camp and they are in danger." She told the dispatcher about her partner's collar. "If you can't track this number, please try to pinpoint Annie's location."

She held the phone away from her ear and made a groaning sound. "I've lost the call." Another try proved futile. "We need to get up higher." She started walking at a fast pace and Jonas scrambled to catch up.

"Do you think they understood anything you said?" His hope was hanging on by a thread.

"Yes, at least part of it. I just hope they'll be able to find us by using Annie's collar because the service on this phone is terrible. It's probably a burner, which means it was prepaid and probably with cash. In other words, it's pretty much untraceable."

The ways of those who did evil were hard to comprehend.

A disturbing thought occurred. The local police were compromised. Was there a chance that there could be a mole in the sheriff's department too? If so, Charlotte had just given away their location as well as Lainey's. He voiced his fears aloud.

Charlotte stopped abruptly and shook her head. "You can trust my team, I promise. The fact that this case seems to trace back to the local police tells me the sheriff's department may be our only hope to set things right. Please trust me, Jonas."

He did trust her. "I do. Always."

She smiled. "I'll keep trying to reach the dispatcher again."

The steep incline of the rising mountain range reminded Jonas of the precarious trek they'd be forced to make. This wasn't the easiest route to reach the location of the house Harley claimed he owned, but with all the activity circling through the woods it was their only choice.

Once they'd cleared most of the trees, the wind whipped around with a force that threatened to knock them over.

But the biggest concern for Jonas was there would be no place to hide should they come across others from Harley's organization.

Jonas looped his arm through Charlotte's to keep them both from stumbling in the brutal wind. They leaned into it and struggled to move.

Out in front of them, Annie turned her head in the direction they'd come and sniffed the air.

Jonas whipped around. Flashlights appeared.

"It looks like it's coming from the location we left those men."

Which meant their partners would have found them and been told the direction he and Charlotte were heading. They were out in the open with no place to hide and a virtual army coming after them.

The phone in Charlotte's pocket chimed an unknown ringtone. Charlotte grabbed it, no doubt thinking the call was from the sheriff. "I don't recognize this number." Her attention shot to Jonas.

"Can Harley's organization track the phone?"

Abruptly the ringtone stopped. "Normally, I'd say no, but this appears to be a sophisticated organization." She stared at the phone in her hand. "We can't afford to keep the phone if there's the slightest chance, they'll be able to track it. I just hope they aren't able to do the same with the phone Lainey and Abram have."

The thought was alarming.

Her gaze slid past Jonas to the flashlights that appeared to be heading straight for their location. "I just hope that Ruby, the dispatcher, was able to understand where Abram and Lainey are, and I hope she heard the part about tracking Annie's GPS collar." She tossed the phone away. It landed some distance down the mountainside. "Is there another path to Harley's?"

"If we head to the right slightly it will be easier going but we'll have to circle back once we summit, which means it will take us longer to reach the place."

Charlotte watched the lights advancing once more. "Let's do it. I just hope those men have no idea about Harley's mountain place, because if so, they'll come after us there."

Jonas shifted their direction. Something soft and wet fell on his face and he looked up and realized it was snowing. Snow covered the ground at their feet. At this high an elevation, the snow sometimes stuck around into summer.

After they'd traveled for some distance, Jonas stopped her. Charlotte gave the command for Annie to halt.

"What's going on?"

"The last time I was up this way was a while ago. Still, we should be safe to start heading for the mountain summit from here." Jonas started toward the dark shapes looming in the distance while the snow swirled harder around them. Temperatures had plummeted. Both he and Charlotte were exhausted.

"My cabin is close," he said. "We can get out of the weather for a bit before continuing."

Charlotte nodded while huddling under her jacket. "So far, it doesn't appear as if they're tracking us, but with the snow on the ground, if they come this way, they'll see our footprints." She pointed to the clear prints behind them.

She was right, but at this point there wasn't much they could do to cover them. "Let's hope the snow fills them in soon."

The darkness and the weather made each step dangerous. The rocks beneath the snow were slippery. One false move and they could be in trouble.

"Give me your hand," Jonas said, and Charlotte looked at him strangely. He pointed to the rocks. "Just to be safe."

She held her hand out to him and he clasped it. The fact that it felt right holding her hand was something he refused to think about.

Annie slowly picked her way through the rocks up higher.

Several times he and Charlotte slipped and almost slid backward.

"How much longer?" Charlotte asked once they stopped to catch their breaths.

He tried to gather his bearings. "Another mile or so."

The dejection on her face confirmed she was struggling.

"Over there." He pointed to a group of rocks that they could get behind to act as a barrier from the wind. "It's a bit of protection until we can catch our breaths and keep going."

With her hand still in his they made their way precariously there. Charlotte knelt beside him. The dog came over and sat on her haunches.

Jonas gathered Charlotte close. She tucked her face against his chest. Over the blowing wind, he was content to hold her and listen for any sound above the quick beat of his heart at having her close.

He rested his chin against her auburn hair, needing a moment of comfort during a night that felt never-ending. This was wrong. How could he have feelings for this woman in his arms when he missed Ivy with every breath?

THIRTEEN

Amidst the confusion in her head, another sound just about broke her heart. Were those footsteps?

Please, God, no.

She focused intently to confirm the worst possible news and it soon became clear. Someone else was up on the mountain.

Charlotte lifted her head and whispered against Jonas's ear. "There's someone up here."

His eyes locked with hers. "Where?"

Getting a correct bead on the direction was difficult in such weather, but she pointed above them while giving Annie the command of silence.

Charlotte held on to Jonas and prayed with all her heart that they wouldn't be spotted. She wasn't sure how much more she could handle. Above everything she wanted them to live. Wanted to save those women if they could. Wanted to make those who were responsible pay.

Over the rush of the wind, the footsteps sounded closer. She clutched Jonas tighter and looked to

Annie who was waiting for her command to attack. Charlotte put her finger on her lips and shook her head. The dog understood. Annie was one of the best K-9 partners she'd ever had, and they worked seamlessly together.

Soon, the noise of crunching footsteps appeared to fade.

Charlotte held Jonas's gaze until the sound was gone completely. "Could you tell how many there were?"

He shook his head.

Pulling in a breath, Charlotte slowly rose. "I don't see anyone."

Jonas stood beside her. "They weren't using flashlights."

"Let's get to your cabin." The cold bored right through to her bones. "Which way?"

Jonas pointed straight ahead. Thankfully, the direction was heading away from whoever was up here on the mountain with them.

Snow mixed with ice fell harder the higher they climbed. Snowflakes clung to Charlotte's lashes, making it hard to see. She brushed a frozen hand across her eyes.

"Over there."

Charlotte squinted through the deluge and spotted the shadow of a structure amongst the darkness. Relief swept through her weakened limbs. If she'd had the strength to run toward it, she would have.

She clutched Jonas's hand and waded through the deep accumulation of snow until they reached the cabin.

Jonas faced her. "Stay here and let me check the cabin out first."

Her teeth were chattering so much it was impossible to get words out.

Jonas shoved the door open and went inside before she could respond. Charlotte wasn't about to let him risk danger alone. She followed him inside the single room and pulled out the flashlight. A cot in the corner. A table and a couple of chairs against one wall. A woodstove proved to be the best thing she'd seen in a while.

"I'll make a fire. It's risky, but we need to warm up. We're both frozen." Jonas opened the woodstove's door and placed some paper inside before adding some wood from a pile stacked close to the stove. He struck a match and soon the paper caught followed by the logs.

Charlotte stood beside him while Annie roamed around the room sniffing.

Jonas dragged the two chairs over close to the fire. "We can't stay long, but it'll be so nice to rest for a little while and warm up."

"Who do you think was out there?" she asked. She couldn't let go of the sensation that whoever it was, they posed a threat, and if the smoke from the fire was spotted…

"There are other trappers who come up here, but most would use a light to see where they were going."

That point gnawed at her brain. "How close are we to the house?"

"Very, though with the weather, finding it might be difficult. It's in a secluded location."

Of course, Harley would choose a place of isolation. Considering that everything pointed to it being a place for illegal activities…trafficking and who knew what else.

She held her hands close to the fire, basking in the warmth of the flames. "I can feel my hands again."

Jonas turned his head her way and smiled. "Me, too. Neither of us exactly dressed for the things we've gone through today."

Charlotte agreed. "I had no idea when I agreed to help Dottie find her granddaughter that I'd almost die and be thrown into the middle of a trafficking ring." Or that she would be teamed up with Jonas…and that being close to him would bring unwelcome reminders of the things she once had in her life.

His smile suddenly disappeared. "I'm glad I found you," he said softly. The roughness in his voice sent a shiver through her. She was glad she had him with her, too. Glad...

Jonas leaned closer and brushed back strands of her hair from her face. "This is the first time in a long time I've felt needed."

She reached for his hand and entwined their fingers. "You are needed, Jonas. I couldn't do this without you. I would have died and so would Lainey."

He studied their joined hands. "These past six years, well, I've been living in a state of self-imposed reclusion because I thought I deserved to be punished for not being there for my wife."

She shook her head before he finished. "You didn't do anything wrong. You were trying to provide for your wife and child. Ivy knew this. You couldn't have predicted what happened..." She was ready to accept that truth for herself, too. She'd spent the last year blaming herself for asking Ryan to come out to assist with the search and yet Ryan wasn't the type of man to sit by when he was needed. It didn't matter if he was sick, he would have come to assist. It was just who he was.

"We've both been blaming ourselves for something that wasn't our fault," he said softly, and she couldn't take her eyes off him. Maybe he was ready to accept the truth, too. She'd been living in limbo for so long, wishing for things that were gone forever.

Jonas leaned forward and touched his forehead to hers. "I'm tired of blaming myself."

A tiny sob escaped her. She was, too. So tired. His lips brushed hers. She inched away for a second, lowering her lashes. Jonas's gentle kiss took her by surprise. But then Charlotte leaned into him and kissed him back.

Unfinished business... The words played on a loop through her mind. She had to uncover the truth. Had to see the face of the person who'd claimed Ryan's life if she were ever going to move forward.

She ended the kiss and straightened. The hurt on Jonas's face confirmed he didn't understand the reason for her sudden change.

He turned away. She tried to come up with the right words to say, but a noise outside had her on sudden alert.

Annie growled and leaped to her feet, moving closer to the door.

Jonas jerked toward the door. There was no lock on it.

Charlotte quieted Annie. "Over there." Charlotte, Jonas and the dog moved to the side of the door. If someone came in, the door would offer them protection and hopefully give them the edge they'd need to overpower the intruder.

Seconds ticked by. Jonas looked her way. She wanted to say so much—to tell him she had feelings for him—yet once more the danger facing them stood in the way.

Someone pounded on the door. "Help me, please. Somebody."

Jonas' eyes widened at the woman's voice. "It's Betty."

He started for the door, but Charlotte stopped him. "What if it's a trick?" she whispered. At this point they couldn't afford to take any chances. Charlotte spotted the back door. "I'll go around and make sure she's alone."

Jonas rejected the idea. "It's too dangerous. Let me."

Though her confidence had taken a beating after everything they'd gone through tonight, she was still a deputy and it fell to her to protect him.

She shook her head. "I'll go. Wait here." Charlotte slipped from the cabin and took a second to listen before proceeding. The person at the front door continued to beg for help. If Betty was alone, Charlotte wanted to get her help as quickly as possible, but she had to make sure Harley—or worse, all those men who had been searching for them—wasn't waiting nearby to ambush.

She slipped quickly around the back to the side of the house and stayed as close to it as she could with the snowdrifts piled up there.

Once Charlotte reached the front of the cabin, she took stock on the limited line of sight. There was a single person huddled near the front door. Nothing else stirred. Betty appeared to be alone.

Charlotte eased toward the woman, trying not to startle her. As she neared, Betty whirled around and screamed. Before she could run away, Charlotte closed the space between them.

"Betty, it's okay," Charlotte said. "I'm a sheriff's deputy. I just had to make sure you were alone."

Betty backed away as she neared. "Why are you up here alone?" Betty was clearly suspicious. The woman didn't have a coat and her feet were bare. She had to be frozen.

"I'm not alone. Jonas Knowles, your neighbor, is inside." Charlotte moved past Betty to the door. "Jonas, it's okay. Betty is alone. We're coming in." She reached for the door, but it opened before she could turn the knob.

Jonas's attention shot between the two women before he stepped back.

Charlotte ushered Betty inside and closed the door. Annie stood in the middle of the room watching with her hackles raised.

"It's okay, Annie. She's a friend." Charlotte put her arm around Betty's shoulders and led her over to one of the chairs. "Sit down and warm yourself. It's freezing outside."

Betty seemed in a state of shock, but she obeyed. "Jonas, why are you here?"

"Never mind that now." Jonas removed his jacket and placed it over Betty's frail shoulders.

Charlotte moved the second chair closer so Betty could put her legs up on it and warm her feet.

As the fire worked its wonders, Betty rocked slightly and moaned. Charlotte found the bottle of water and opened the cap before handing it to Betty. "Here, drink it slowly."

Betty stared at the bottle as if she didn't understand. Charlotte held the bottle to her lips, and she eventually drank a few sips.

Charlotte felt the woman's hands. They were still ice-cold but the heat from the stove was slowly melting the chill away. She took off her firemen's coat and placed it over Betty's legs and feet, noticing there were fresh cut marks on her hands. Charlotte's mouth thinned as she thought about the terrible things Harley had put this innocent woman through. Betty probably didn't have any family to turn to for help, and Harley was good at intimidating those weaker than himself.

Her fear for the young women with Harley grew, and Charlotte wanted to jump in and ask Betty how she'd ended up here on the mountain where they were searching for her husband. Yet the look of bewilderment on Betty's face told her Betty had nothing to do with her husband's crimes.

A deep, gut-wrenching sigh escaped Betty's lips, and she focused on Jonas as if she were really seeing him. "Jonas, I'm glad you're here." A tiny smile hovered at the corners of her lips.

Jonas knelt beside her. "Are you hurt?" he asked gently. Her hands were cut up as if she'd been in a fight.

Betty's eyes filled with tears, but she shook her head. "I'm okay. I got these running through the underbrush near the cabin."

Jonas frowned. "Near this cabin or…"

The words were barely out before she shook her head. "No, not this cabin. The one Harley just told me about."

Jonas's eyes slid to Charlotte. She appeared just as confused as him.

"You didn't have any idea Harley had a place up here?"

Betty wiped her eyes. "No, he's never said a word about a house in the mountains. I never even realized he came up here."

Charlotte moved to the other side of Jonas, drawing Betty's attention.

"I recognize you," the woman said.

"You do?" Charlotte asked in surprise, and

Jonas wondered if Betty had been at the house when Charlotte was attacked.

"Yes, you came to the house before…to talk to Harley."

Jonas remembered the times Charlotte had gone to the house on a domestic violence report.

Charlotte smiled gently. "That's right. I was at your house earlier today—yesterday. In the afternoon. Were you home?"

Betty stared at her with a frown creasing her forehead. "Why, no. Harley sent me to Bozeman for supplies."

Charlotte frowned. Bozeman was over a hundred miles away. Why would Harley send her so far to get supplies…? He wanted her out of the house so he could handle his illegal activity.

"Why were you at my house?"

Charlotte looked at Jonas before answering. "I came there looking for my friend, Lainey Marques. Her grandmother called and asked for mine and Annie's help." She indicated the dog. "Annie followed Lainey's trail to your house."

Betty looked at the animal but still didn't understand. "And you found her there?"

Charlotte shook her head. "She needs to hear the truth," she told Jonas.

Jonas agreed. Betty needed to see what her husband was capable of. "Tell her."

Charlotte drew in a breath and told her about

what happened to her after she'd reached Harley's house. "Your husband tried to kill me and Lainey. Since then, we've been trying to escape armed men who are working with Harley." She paused before telling Betty about the young women who Lainey reported being held at their house.

Jonas watched Betty's expression carefully for any sign she might have been involved in her husband's crimes.

Her hand flew up to cover her trembling lips. "They were there—at my house? I had no idea, but it explains why Harley sent me away from the house so often. He must have brought them there while I was away and made sure they were gone before I returned."

Jonas sat back on his haunches and watched Betty's pained reaction. "You know about the girls?" He couldn't accept she was part of Harley's evil plans.

Betty repeatedly shook her head. "No, I didn't, not until Harley brought them up here a little while ago."

"Harley's here with the girls?" Charlotte asked in shock. "When did this happen?"

Betty clutched her hands together in her lap. "About an hour earlier."

Relief sank in quickly. The girls were alive. At least for the moment. "Why don't you start by telling us how you ended up here," Jonas said quietly.

Betty gave a shuddering sigh. "As I said, Harley told me to go to Bozeman to get supplies."

"Does he do this often?" Jonas rarely saw Betty outside the house.

"No," she replied, "usually only a couple of times a month. He sends me there with a list of things he needs, and he tells me not to come back home until I call first."

Harley wanted to make sure Betty wasn't around when he was moving the girls.

"What happened yesterday?" Charlotte glanced at the door as if half expecting Harley to barge in.

"It started early—much earlier than normal. Harley was up before dawn. When I woke up, he told me to head to Bozeman. He didn't even allow me to have my breakfast." Betty rubbed her trembling lips. "He's done something terrible, hasn't he?"

"I'm afraid so," Charlotte said quietly. "Please keep going."

"Well, I left immediately. I knew better than to cross him." She trembled as if the thought terrified her. "Anyway, I got the things he needed and was ready to head home, only Harley told me he would call when I could come."

"And did he?" Jonas still couldn't grasp the events that had taken place.

"Yes, but it was afternoon, and when I got home, he told me I had to leave again."

A strange thing. Probably with everything that happened, Harley didn't want Betty anywhere near the house.

"He told me about the house up here in the mountains." Betty's surprise was clear. "I had no idea he had it. Harley told me how to get here and insisted I should take a side-by-side." Her bottom lip quivered. "I didn't even realize he owned a side-by-side. It was parked near a truck I didn't recognize. When I asked him about it, he hit me here—" she touched her cheek "—and told me to mind my own business and not to try anything or he'd come after me."

Jonas's blood boiled at Harley's cruel treatment of his wife.

"So, you did as he asked," Charlotte prompted when Betty grew quiet.

"Yes. I got here after dark, and I was so scared. I'd never been in the mountains at night. Anyway, as soon as I reached the house, Harley called, checking up on me. He told me to wait there until he told me differently."

She stood suddenly when a sound outside grabbed everyone's attention.

"I'll check it out, but I'm pretty sure it was the wind." Charlotte stepped out into the cold. Both

Jonas and Betty didn't take their eyes off the door until she returned.

"There's no sign of anyone. Still, we need to go after the women while we can," Charlotte told Jonas.

"I'm not sure they're still alive," Betty said.

The shock of those words settled uncomfortably around Jonas. "Why do you say such a thing?" Had they risked their lives only to find the women they'd been trying to save were all dead?

FOURTEEN

Charlotte waited with dread for Betty to tell them what she'd witnessed.

"The house was big—bigger than our place. I looked around and realized there were two floors. The one you come in from the front door and then a basement area," Betty explained. "Even though Harley told me not to go downstairs, I did. It was dark and there was a room cluttered with stuff."

"What kind of stuff?" Charlotte asked. She recalled how the basement in the house near Jonas's had been virtually empty.

"All sorts of electronics. Boxes of new cell phones and tablets. Other types of laptops. There were some crates I couldn't open. I have no idea where those things come from. Harley works at the lumber mill from time to time. He insists I stay home and keep the house." Betty lifted her gaze to them. "We live paycheck to paycheck. How was he able to afford all those things?"

Charlotte didn't say as much, but she was

pretty sure all those items were stolen. "What happened when Harley arrived?" She hated to push the already shaken Betty, but time was critical, and she and Jonas had to understand what they'd be facing once they reached the house.

"He stormed in and demanded to know what I'd been up to." Betty's shifting facial expressions showed she was reliving the terror. "I told him nothing. I'm not sure he believed me or not, but he went back outside and brought in four young women."

The girls who had been held with Lainey.

"Did you recognize any of them?" Charlotte asked.

Betty shook her head, her worried eyes holding Charlotte's. "No, I had no idea why they were there. I tried to ask Harley, but he told me to keep my mouth shut and then he took my phone." She wiped at her eyes once more.

"He forced the girls downstairs. When he came back up, he kept muttering something about 'they were going to kill him.' I had no idea what he was talking about but the look on his face scared me. I tried to stay out of his way. He just kept pacing the room and saying he didn't know what to do. After a while, he went outside and was gone for a long time. When he came back in, he stormed back down the stairs and slammed the door. I heard several shots. That's when I ran."

Had Harley murdered those girls? *Please, Lord, let them be alive.*

Another frightening thought occurred. According to the timeline, Harley could have been the one roaming around before she and Jonas reached his cabin.

Clearly, Harley was growing paranoid and worried his people were turning on him—with good reason according to what they'd overheard.

"I tried to use the side-by-side to get away," Betty went on shakily, "only the keys were gone. Harley must have taken them. And there was another side-by-side parked beside it without the key, either."

Harley wanted to make sure she didn't escape. If he killed the young women, he'd do the same to Betty. And when he realized she was gone, he'd come looking for her.

"Betty, you stay here where it's warm. We're going after the women." Charlotte turned to Jonas, beckoning him away. "We need to find a way to secure the doors for her. Just in case," she said in a whisper.

Jonas looked around the cabin. "I can use the table to block the back entrance." He went back to Betty, crouching before her. "Betty, when we step outside, I need you to take one of the chairs and shove it beneath the doorknob. Don't open the door to anyone but us."

Betty grabbed Jonas's arm, her face filled with fear. "He'll kill you if he catches you."

The words had her chest tightening. "We'll be careful. Are you familiar with how to use a weapon?" She moved next to Jonas as he rose.

Betty slowly nodded. "Yes, when I was young, my father taught me."

Charlotte held out one of the handguns. "If someone tries to get in besides us, shoot to kill."

Betty clasped the weapon with a hand that shook. "I almost forgot. I took Harley's phone before I left the house."

"You did?" Jonas said in disbelief.

"Yes. As I was leaving, I grabbed it. He'd left it on the table. Only it wasn't his usual phone. I've never seen this one before." She gave the mobile to Charlotte.

The service indicator confirmed cell reception was nonexistent. The mountain so close was probably blocking any signal.

With Jonas looking over her shoulder, Charlotte scrolled through the numbers called. "Here's one for a D.A. This must be the same D.A. that was mentioned before." Charlotte asked Betty about the person.

Betty shrugged. "I have no idea. I have a suspicion there are lots of things Harley kept from me."

Even if there was no service, the phone could

be used as evidence against Harley. Charlotte shoved it into her pocket. "Are you warm enough?" She and Jonas had the jackets Abram gave them. She'd leave Betty the fire jacket. She'd be okay. Hopefully, the cold would keep them sharp.

Betty nodded. "Yes, I'm fine."

As much as Charlotte wanted to leave Annie there to protect Betty, they'd need her partner's expertise to alert them to danger.

Jonas moved one of the chairs over to the door. "Don't forget to wedge the chair under the doorknob, Betty."

Charlotte checked her magazine. The clip was almost full. "Ready?" she asked him while stuffing the weapon into her pocket. The tension on Jonas's face matched hers.

"We'd better hurry," he said. "If Harley shot those women, then they could be in bad shape."

She stepped past him into the cold weather that had continued to worsen. Once she was sure Betty had secured the door, she and Jonas started walking while Annie took her position as lead.

"How far are we?" Charlotte was on edge, expecting Harley or one of the rest of his crew members to find them. She scanned their surroundings.

"Half an hour under normal circumstances, but in this weather…" He shrugged. It was excruciating to realize the storm berating the mountains would slow them down even more when every second counted. "Harley probably knows Betty escaped by now. He may be out looking for her."

And if he was, with the weather and the darkness, they might not even see him until it was too late.

Jonas replayed every piece of Betty's story in his head. Harley was now desperate and had quite possibly executed the young women he'd brought with him. He wouldn't want to leave any witnesses. Betty was a witness who could not only place the women with Harley but also identify the timeline in which Harley had had her leave the house. Jonas was certain it would match up to when the women had been moved.

"I pray we find them alive." Charlotte voiced the biggest thing on his mind aloud. "Those poor girls. They've been through so much already, and to lose their lives because Harley is worried about getting caught..."

Jonas's hand fisted around his weapon. "Harley is only one man. If we can take him by surprise, we should be able to overpower him. I'm more worried about those other men. If they're tracking Harley's phone, they could be anywhere up here." And Charlotte had the phone. With a virtual army of soldiers bearing down on them, there wouldn't be much time.

"All the more reason to find Harley and subdue him quickly," Charlotte said. "If his back is against the wall then we stand a chance at flipping him."

The Harley Jonas was familiar with wouldn't give in so easily. He'd fight until the bitter end, but he didn't tell Charlotte that.

A sudden unidentified sound had the dog charging ahead.

"Annie, no." Charlotte grabbed the dog's collar before she left their sight. "Come." She and Jonas crouched behind a pile of rocks near the mountainside.

Movement came from nearby. It sounded like more than one person. Were they too late?

"I can't get a read off this thing," a male voice Jonas recognized from one of their previous encounters came from only a few feet away.

"Let me have a look." The second person's voice came closer. "The program's not working. The weather, I'm sure. The last time we were able to get a track on Harley's phone it was somewhere to the left of this location." The man huffed out a breath. "Let's head that way. He told us to take Harley out and then get the girls and evidence Harley has. And I for one don't want to cross him. I've seen what he's capable of with the girl and the dog trainer."

Next to him, Charlotte's shoulders quivered.

Two sets of footsteps carefully shuffled away, the men grumbling at the weather, Harley and what they'd need to do. Soon, the sounds faded.

Annie left her hiding spot and sniffed the ground, picking up the men's scents but not tracking them.

"I'm sorry," Jonas said softly. He brushed her hair away from her face and held her gaze. "But we must hurry, Charlotte. We can't let those men kill Harley and destroy whatever evidence he's been gathering on the person in charge." Jonas rose and pulled her up beside him. "I realize it hurts to hear the truth verified, but those girls are counting on us."

Charlotte drew in a breath and let it go slowly. "You're right." She pulled out Harley's phone. "Right now, they probably aren't able to track the phone due to the weather, but that could change." She turned the phone off. "They shouldn't be able to track it if it's off."

In the distance, daylight lightened the sky. He pointed the dawning out to her.

"As happy as I am to see the sunlight coming, it will make it easier for us to be spotted." She glanced around uneasily. "I sure hope between our call, and Lainey and Abram's, help is on its way. We can't stay hidden much longer."

The edge in her tone confirmed how serious their situation was. The only way out should those men keep coming would be to summit the mountains, and from what Jonas remembered, that would be difficult.

"Hey, I think I see something," Charlotte said. She'd stopped and was leaning forward as if to see better.

Jonas glanced through the troubling weather and saw it, too. "That's the house." He started for it when Charlotte grabbed him.

"What's wrong?"

"Those men are up there somewhere."

What she wasn't saying was the chances were great that he and Charlotte would have to take them down before they were able to search for Harley.

Jonas's blood hummed through his veins, warning him the showdown he'd been expecting for a while was about to take place. They'd survived so much. Could they make it through another battle?

As he looked into her pretty face, there were things he wanted to say. He cupped her shoulders and brought her close. "Charlotte…"

She placed her finger over his lips and didn't let him finish. "We have to end this, Jonas. Nothing else matters. Those girls have families who need to know what happened to them no matter what."

He slowly nodded. She was right. Now was not the time to talk about them. What he'd been about to say could wait.

Slowly they advanced toward the house. The two side-by-sides that Betty had mentioned were parked out front. Why hadn't Harley chosen to flee on one if he suspected those men were searching for him to kill him? Leave the women and use the side-by-side and head over the mountain and out of danger. It didn't make sense unless Harley had been found and killed already.

No.

As bad as Harley was, Jonas wanted him alive to have to pay for what he'd done.

Charlotte pointed to the side of the house. Jonas spotted a man carefully looking around. Was it one of the men they'd overheard earlier? Where was the second man? "We have to take him down as quietly as possible." She held the gun in her hand. "Stay behind me."

She was still trying to protect him.

"Stay, Annie," Charlotte said and moved quickly toward the unsuspecting man. Before they reached his side, he whipped around and opened fire.

Charlotte pulled Jonas behind a nearby tree

before returning fire. Shots rang out all around them. She waited until silence followed and shot at her target. The man screamed and hit the ground.

Jonas followed Charlotte over to the perp. She felt for a pulse. "He's gone." Before they had a chance to move, the second man came around the corner, weapon blazing.

Jonas whirled around and fired. The surprise on the shooter's face before he fell would haunt Jonas the rest of his life. The man was dead.

Charlotte squeezed his arm as if reading his distraught thoughts. "There's no way Harley didn't hear what happened."

Jonas forced the regret back and followed her to the back of the house. Betty had been right. There was no rear entrance. The house butted up against the mountainside.

Annie moved closer, likely to protect her partner.

If Harley was inside, he'd have seen their approach through the front windows.

"What do we do?" Jonas asked. He was at a loss and his exhausted brain was making it hard to think clearly.

"Most houses have two entrances. There must be another entrance on the other side."

The question was how they got there without alerting Harley they were coming.

"Follow me," Charlotte said and eased back to the front of the house.

Once they reached it, she pointed to the porch. "If we can duck down low enough, the porch should protect us from anyone inside's line of sight."

It was risky, but everything they'd done up until this point had been risky.

Jonas nodded and bent down low following Charlotte's example.

With his heartbeat drowning out all other sound, he hurried after Charlotte until they reached the other side of the house.

Another door.

Charlotte edged toward the nearby window and looked inside. "It's a kitchen."

Jonas got on the opposite side of the pane and tried to see as much as possible. A small kitchen, then a living room. On the opposite wall of the kitchen was a door. Which must be the door leading downstairs to the basement where Harley had taken the women.

"I don't see anyone." Charlotte waited for him to confirm. "It's possible Harley is searching for Betty and not here. If that's the case, we won't have long." She shifted back to the door and eased toward it.

Jonas's hands were shaking. After everything

they'd gone through, it felt as if they were at the end of the road one way or another.

"Annie, stay here and watch." The dog's ears tilted to alert. She understood and would be on guard.

Charlotte tried the doorknob. It turned in her hands. She shot Jonas a look that was filled with apprehension. She slowly twisted it open and stepped inside with her weapon drawn.

Jonas kept close to her. She might be law enforcement, but he would have her back no matter what.

In the kitchen, Jonas quietly closed the door. The house didn't appear to be occupied. His gut twisted. The girls.

"We have to clear this floor first," Charlotte told him. This was police procedure and part of her training.

They moved through the few rooms on that floor. Living room, kitchen, bedroom and bath. Each room was cluttered and appeared as if the person who was staying there had little regard for neatness.

A reminder of Harley's messy yard. But the house down the mountain had been kept up thanks to Betty. Her touches were not present here. Betty had said she had no idea Harley had a place up on the mountain and that appeared to be true.

"There's no one here," Charlotte confirmed as they returned to the living room. There was a woodstove in the middle of the space. She pointed to it. "That hasn't been used in a while."

"You're right. Probably not in a long time. So, Betty was here for a while with no heat?"

She shrugged. "He may have told her not to use it. But why would he do so unless..." Charlotte hurried over to the stove and opened the door. "The ashes are cold." She dug around. "There's something here." She pulled out a phone. "It's mine and there's another one. This is Lainey's." She turned the phones over. "The batteries have been removed," she said in a dejected tone. "He was making sure they couldn't be tracked." Charlotte handed both phones to Jonas. "There's something else here. A book."

Charlotte pulled it out and flipped through its pages.

"It's girls' names, descriptions and dates."

Jonas looked over her shoulder at the names before confirming what she was likely thinking. "He wrote down the captured girls' descriptions and names."

Charlotte flipped through page after page. "This has been going on for at least five years. Probably longer. Harley didn't wise up and start keeping notes until then."

"Too bad he didn't list the names of those involved," Jonas said, recalling the conversation he and Charlotte had overheard.

"This isn't what the person in charge was looking for," she said mostly to herself. "If Harley went to this much trouble to list the names of the girls, why wouldn't he also name his accomplices in case he was caught? He'd have leverage." Understanding dawned on her face. "He took the evidence that the man in charge is worried about with him," Charlotte concluded.

"Perhaps." But why take some and not everything?

Charlotte flipped through the remaining pages. On the inside cover at the back, Harley had taped a key. "Wait, this looks like a safe deposit key or a personal safe. Maybe there's one in the basement?" She faced him. "Stay close." They returned to the kitchen. She placed her ear on the door and listened. "I don't hear anything."

The words held little comfort when the reason they'd come here was to save the young women.

Charlotte's hand hovered over the door handle. "Ready?" she asked him, but he could see that she wasn't nearly ready to face whatever waited for them downstairs.

"Yes, I'm ready," he told her. "It will be okay." He didn't elaborate, likely doing a poor job of reassuring her.

Charlotte nodded and reached for the handle.

"It's locked." She shot him a look before focusing on the keyhole in the center of the knob.

If Harley had left to look for Betty, he might have secured the door in case someone was to happen upon the house. But what was he hiding behind the lock?

"Stand back." Charlotte took the butt of her weapon and slammed it against the knob. It took half a dozen tries before the knob broke off. The door still wouldn't open.

"Let me." Jonas put his full weight against the door, and it eventually gave way.

Darkness and bitter cold flew up to greet them.

Jonas tried the light switch without any response. The lights would probably be powered by a generator, which obviously wasn't working.

He pulled out the flashlight and clicked it, shining it down the steps to the floor below. From his limited line of sight, the space appeared cluttered with boxes.

"Stay close," Charlotte repeated and started down the steps, using her flashlight in one hand to guide her and the handgun at the ready in the other.

Jonas glanced over his shoulder, expecting Harley to appear out of the blue and attack them.

He wasn't normally one for jumping at shadows, but the last hours they'd spent trying to allude people who were trying to kill them had taught him that not being aware of his surroundings could cost lives.

Charlotte stopped abruptly when one of the stairs squeaked. She blew out a breath that chilled the air in front of her. "Let's keep going." She slowly covered the remaining steps until she stood on the basement floor.

Jonas stopped next to her. The space was filled with boxes and what appeared to be other types of electronics and expensive phones and tablets like Betty had described.

"Where did he get all of this?" Jonas asked as he flashed the light around the clutter.

"He probably stole it. Or someone else did and it's a form of payment for getting the girls."

Jonas's mouth thinned. Harley had been up to terrible things.

Moving through the clutter was difficult. Jonas shoved boxes out of the way just to have a place to walk.

He and Charlotte slowly fanned out and searched every corner of the room. His worst fear was he'd find the bodies of the young women among the boxes, or that Harley was just waiting for him to make a wrong move to take him out.

Something moved out of the corner of his eye and Jonas whirled toward it. He realized it was a rat the size of a small dog. The sight of the rodent gave him the creeps.

He kept searching until he reached one wall. There was a door. Jonas drew in a breath and slowly pulled the door open. A small closet stuffed with more electronics greeted him. He bent over in relief.

"Anything?" Charlotte called out from beyond the stacks of boxes.

"Nothing but a rat. What about you?"

"There's no sign of them… Wait, I see something."

Jonas hurried over as fast as the clutter would allow. "What is it?"

"Bullet holes." She pointed to the wall. "I count at least three and there are several more lodged in the boxes." She flashed the light all around. "But there's no sign of blood."

Which meant Harley hadn't hit those young women with his shots. Had he been trying to scare them or simply on the verge of a breakdown and out of control?

FIFTEEN

"Where are they?" Charlotte glanced around the crowded space before turning the key over in her hand. "And what does this fit?"

"Whatever it is, I don't believe it's down here. We should head back upstairs. It's freezing down here."

She agreed and started for the steps when a sound caught her attention. "Did you hear that?" The sound came again. "A whimper."

Charlotte hurried toward the noise. "It's coming from inside the wall. Hello?" she called. "Who's there?"

"Help! Please, help us!" A young woman's frantic voice came from nearby.

"I'm Deputy Charlotte Walker. How did you get in there?"

"There's a hidden door," the muffled voice replied. "He tapped the wall and it opened."

Charlotte and Jonas both began knocking on the wall.

"Wait, I have something." Jonas felt around the wide crack in between boards. "Got it." He yanked hard and the hidden door opened.

Four frightened women were tied to hooks on the wall.

"Help us," the same woman cried out while others whimpered, clearly too afraid to speak.

All four shivered from fear and the cold, their eyes huge and terrified.

"We've got you," Charlotte told the vocal woman and, with Jonas's help, worked to untie the leather straps that secured the women to the hooks. "Where did Harley go?" she asked the one who'd spoken before.

Once she was loose, the young woman rubbed her wrists. "I'm not sure. I heard him rummaging around and then he went upstairs but he hasn't returned."

"What's your name?" Charlotte asked.

"I'm Elizabeth. This is Sally, Jennifer and Maria." She pointed to each of the freed women. "Please, you have to get us out of here before he comes back."

Charlotte uttered a silent prayer of thanks that they'd been able to find the women.

"She's right," she told Jonas. "We'll take them to Betty and then return because I can't help but sense there are answers here somewhere."

Charlotte led the way up the stairs all the while expecting Harley to waylay them.

"Did you find the other girl?" Elizabeth asked once they reached the landing and gathered in the kitchen.

"You mean another girl who was with you at the first house?" Charlotte asked.

Elizabeth shook her head. "No, she was here with us earlier. She said her name was Sasha."

Shocked, Charlotte jerked toward Jonas. "That's the name of the girl Michaela reported."

"She showed up here after the older woman left," Elizabeth explained. "I heard her and Harley get into this terrible argument and then I heard her scream."

"He must have taken her with him," Jonas said. "Let's get these women to my cabin and out of danger."

Charlotte slipped outside the side door and checked to make sure it was safe before ushering the women outside. "Stay close. We have no idea where Harley is," she warned. Charlotte gave the word for Annie to follow.

Every step of the way to Jonas's cabin was filled with apprehension.

As they neared, Charlotte called out to Betty. "It's us, Betty. Open the door." She searched their surroundings to make sure Harley hadn't followed them.

Sounds of the chair being moved were followed by the door opening. When Betty spotted the girls, she clasped her hand over her mouth. "I was so worried...so afraid he'd killed you."

Charlotte followed the women inside with Jonas. "We can't stay." She explained about the key they'd found. "Do you have any idea what it might fit?"

"I'm not sure," Betty told her, "but I do remember Harley kept eyeing the bookcase when he found me down in the basement, as if he didn't want me near it."

Charlotte squeezed Betty's arm. "Thank you. Take care of the girls."

Once the chair was back in place, Charlotte called the dog, and they hiked the distance back to Harley's mountain house. It felt quicker this time, knowing where they were going, and that Harley's captives were safe. She'd even forgotten about the cold, though the snow kept falling.

They were so close to this being over...just a little bit farther.

"I wonder if there's a safe behind the bookcase...or if the key is to a door," Charlotte said. "The way Harley was able to escape with Sasha. What's her part in all this?"

He frowned. "No doubt she was a victim in the beginning, like you said, and probably agreed to help Harley to stay alive."

As they reached Harley's house, the dog served as lookout again as they entered through the side door once more. Charlotte started back downstairs. "We have to find out what's behind the bookcase."

She pulled the key free of its tape and kept the book with names with her as she hurried down the steps once more.

Jonas followed her down the stairs.

Charlotte reached the bookcase, which held a handful of outdated books. "I didn't notice this before. There's a space between the bookcase and the wall. Help me move it."

With Jonas's help, they were able to inch the heavy piece of furniture away enough to see behind it.

"A door!" Jonas exclaimed. It stood slightly ajar as if someone had been in a rush and had forgotten to close it.

Charlotte flashed the light into what appeared to be a tunnel with a low ceiling. "I don't like this," she whispered with trepidation washing over her.

Jonas let out a breath. "If Harley used the tunnel to escape, he could be long gone by now."

Charlotte slipped inside with Jonas right behind her. The space was dank. "These look like footprints." Charlotte zeroed the light in on the ground where multiple prints were embedded in the dust. "Someone's been down this tunnel recently."

She had a bad feeling, and yet if there was a chance at catching Harley, they had to go after him. "Let's keep going." She bent down so that she could move. Jonas remained close behind her. They had only taken a few steps when a noise behind them had Charlotte turning. "Someone's here."

Jonas jerked toward the sound. Something was tossed inside, and the door slammed shut. Charlotte recognized the object immediately. "It's a grenade. Run, Jonas!" She whipped around and started running, Jonas right on top of her.

They'd managed only a handful of steps when an explosion rocked the world around them. Charlotte lost her footing and fell to the dirt. Jonas placed his body over her to protect her as the explosion reduced the tunnel in the direction they'd come to rubble. Ashen dust flew down, covering everything, including them.

Charlotte coughed, trying to clear the dust from her lungs. They both sat up. "Are you okay?" she asked.

He was covered in white, and the dust reduced him to a fit of coughing, which was concerning.

"Jonas?" She couldn't find her flashlight.

"I'm okay," he wheezed and shoved the rubble that had landed on them away. "There's the light." He grabbed it and shone it around to reveal the devastation. Part of the ceiling had collapsed along with half the tunnel. Every second they were here they were in danger of the rest of it collapsing. Somehow, Harley had been able to hide from them until they were inside and then he'd taken advantage of the situation to try to kill them.

"The evidence. I lost it in the collapse."

Jonas flashed the light around until he located the book. "Here." He handed it to Charlotte.

"Thank goodness." She'd tucked both phones and the key into her pocket. They were safe inside—she wouldn't lose track of them until they were in the sheriff's hands.

More rumbling sounded as pieces of the tunnel continued to break away.

"It's not safe here. We need to see where this tunnel leads," Jonas told her. He slowly rose as far as he could and helped Charlotte up.

The ground beneath them shook violently. "This whole place is going to collapse. We'll need to reach the end before that happens."

Another rumble had her stumbling. She grabbed hold of Jonas and together they held on until the moment passed. A blast of debris flew all around them.

"Run!" Charlotte yelled again when she looked

over her shoulder and couldn't see anything but a dust cloud.

She raced down the tunnel with the flashlight's beam picking up nothing but gray.

Over the rumbles of aftershocks, keeping their feet beneath them was next to impossible. She prayed there was a way out at the end of the tunnel, and that Harley hadn't destroyed it before trying to kill them. If so, they'd be buried here along with Harley's secrets.

Jonas couldn't see an end in sight. The dust was so thick, and every breath he took tasted like ash.

"I can't imagine this can go on much farther," Charlotte managed before coughing violently.

"We need to cover our noses and mouths." Jonas ripped off more of his lining and handed her a strip. The inside of his jacket had become completely frayed. "It's not much, but it might help."

Charlotte stopped long enough to tie the cloth over her nose and mouth. "It helps."

Jonas did the same and they started moving again. How had the tunnel come to be in the first place? Though he wasn't acquainted with Harley beyond what he'd seen him do to Betty, and what he'd heard from Charlotte, his neighbor didn't seem the type to put a lot of hard labor into doing something like this.

"Do you suppose Harley built the tunnel?" he asked Charlotte. She had slowed down. Despite covering their noses and mouths, it was still difficult breathing, and the struggle was slowing them down.

"No way. I'm not sure this house even belongs to Harley. It seems likely that this tunnel was made on the orders of whoever's heading up the trafficking ring as a way to move girls." She steadied herself as another blast rocked the ground.

Charlotte breathed deeply. "But who knows… It's hard to think clearly."

He felt the same way. He could feel his body slowing down from the miles of walking and this final blow.

"This place gives me the creeps," Charlotte said with a shudder. "It seems almost as if we're living on borrowed time."

Jonas felt the same way. He prayed they reached the end before the whole thing collapsed.

A crashing noise up ahead had him stopping. "What was that?"

Charlotte stood beside him and waited. "I don't know but I don't like the sound of it."

A few minutes later, the sound of an engine

firing overhead could be heard. "It must be Harley. He's leaving."

"Let's keep going," Charlotte said. "The only way to get help is to get out of here alive."

As they continued walking, a scent much stronger than the dust reached them.

"Is it…?" Charlotte whirled around and stared up at him, wide-eyed.

"Smoke." He voiced it in utter disbelief. Harley had set the place on fire. "If the collapsing tunnel isn't enough, he's going to burn us alive."

The terror on her face made him wish he'd chosen his words better. "We still have a chance," he told her and placed his hands on her shoulders. "We keep fighting. We don't give up."

Charlotte slowly nodded. "You're right. This tunnel is safe from the fire, unless it can penetrate the compromised areas…"

"We aren't sure that's happened."

Still, the smoke from above was mingling with the dust and making it impossible to breathe. Soon, it wouldn't matter if the fire could reach them. The smoke they were inhaling would kill them.

They kept moving as fast as they could to stay ahead of the rumbles that continued to shake the collapsing tunnel. Jonas tried not to give in to the fear that gripped him—they just needed to focus on getting out.

"I see something." Jonas focused the light ahead. "That looks like a door." She ran toward it and he followed.

They reached for the door handle and realized it was locked from the outside.

"Oh, no." Charlotte shoved her weight against it. "It won't budge."

Behind them, the smoke grew thicker. "Let's see if we can get the doorknob loose and hopefully the door will open." Jonas followed Charlotte's earlier example and slammed the butt of the handgun against the handle. It gave way eventually, only the door didn't open. He threw his weight against it. "Something's blocking it."

Charlotte took the flashlight and shone it through the hole where the doorknob used to be. "I can't see anything." She straightened. "I'm certain Harley put something in front of the door. Something heavy."

In other words, if they couldn't get the door open, they were stuck here with no way to escape. His chest tightened—they were running out of time.

"Let's see if we can work together and get it open," he said with a calm he didn't feel. Jonas placed his shoulder against the door and waited for Charlotte to do the same.

"On the count of three." He counted off and

they worked together to shove against the door. Nothing happened.

"This isn't working," Charlotte said, her voice rising. "We're stuck, Jonas." She searched his face. "We'll have to try and go back the way we came. Let's see if we can move the debris out of the way."

They both knew the odds of getting through the rubble was next to impossible, but she was right. If they remained here and did nothing, they'd be dead.

SIXTEEN

Charlotte's legs were rubber. Walking took all the strength she could muster, but there wasn't any other option. If they didn't try, death was certain.

She kept close behind Jonas. Every little rumble had her cringing and thinking this could be the one that ended it all.

As they headed back down the tunnel, the smoke grew thicker. Both she and Jonas were coughing hard, their eyes watering so much, it was hard to see.

She tapped his shoulder. "We need to dampen the rags." She pointed to the cloth covering her mouth and nose. "It should help us breathe and keep some of the smoke out."

Charlotte pulled out her bottled water she'd taken from the fire tower from her jacket pocket and wet the cloth while Jonas did the same.

It helped some, or maybe she just wanted it to be better.

They reached the first pile of rubble, which completely blocked the path ahead.

Jonas began moving the rocks. Charlotte moved to his side and assisted until there was enough room to crawl over the remaining rocks.

Jonas went first. Once he'd reached the other side, he held out his hand for Charlotte. "You can do it."

Though it sounded as if Harley was heading away from their location, she was still worried he would somehow find Betty and the girls. They had to make it out of here. Charlotte told Jonas about her fears.

He shook his head. "Harley's too worried about saving himself to go back for them."

She got down on her hands and knees and crawled through the opening with his help.

"One down," she said and attempted a laugh to lighten the moment.

"Let's hope there aren't too many more."

Tension coiled through her body. Having to walk almost doubled over and breathing in a mixture of dust and smoke was taking its toll. Her back ached. Her eyes burned and teared up. And her lungs felt as if they were clogged.

Another pile of debris lay ahead of them. The heat from the fire above had grown intense.

"I sure hope we're not walking into the fire," Jonas said.

So far, the light hadn't picked up any flames, but then she had no idea what would lay on the other side of the debris field.

Charlotte touched her hand to it. "I don't feel heat."

Together they worked to free a space to pass through.

Once they were on the other side, Charlotte shone the light all around. They were close to the door they'd entered.

After working their way around another mountain of rocks, Charlotte stood before the door.

Once more, she felt it to see if it was safe. "It's cool to the touch." She looked under the door but there was no sign of smoke.

"Let's try it," Jonas said. He attempted to push the door open but something was blocking it.

"It's the bookcase." Charlotte joined him and they tried to push the door open.

"This is more than the bookcase," Jonas said. "It's like something has been nailed over the door to prevent it from opening... Harley did this. He wants us to die down here." He stepped back and looked at the path they'd come. "I'm not sure what to do."

Charlotte reached for his hand. "We pray."

His eyes held hers. "You're right. We've done everything we could. *Gott* is the only One who can save us now."

Clutching his hand, Charlotte poured out her heart to God. "We need You, Lord. We're all out of options as far as we can see through human eyes, but we know that You can get us through this. We wait on You, Lord. Please help us. Amen."

Though their circumstances hadn't changed yet, they wouldn't die here. God had a plan for them, and it wasn't to die here in this tunnel.

"There's no way out here, we have to go back," Charlotte said. "We have nothing to lose at this point."

Together she and Jonas scrambled back toward the other end of the tunnel. They knew how to maneuver around the debris this time. As they neared, barking came from beyond the door. Had the fire gone out? The barking was the best sound ever. "That's Annie. She's found her way to the end of the tunnel." Once Charlotte reached the door, she called out to her partner. "Annie, get help. We need you to get help."

The dog barked again but she didn't move.

"She's not responding," Jonas said.

Charlotte's heart sank. Annie wasn't leaving her behind. Her eyes filled with tears, and she sank down to her knees. "Annie, it's okay." She loved the dog and couldn't bear the thought of dying and leaving her alone.

Jonas knelt beside her and took her in his arms. She wrapped her arms around him and held him tight. "Jonas, I'm so sorry." She was crying but it felt right. The emotions that had been boiling up inside her were finally free.

"Don't…" he murmured and tipped her chin back. "I'd do it all over again."

Charlotte pushed her mask aside and lowered his. If this was the end for them, she wanted to kiss him one more time.

She leaned forward and touched her lips to his. A sob escaped and the dam released. She kissed him with everything in her heart.

Jonas placed his hands on either side of her head and kissed her back.

The dog continued barking and then another sound had them breaking apart.

"What was that?" Charlotte asked.

It took her a few seconds to realize it was the sound of someone near the door.

"There's someone out there," Jonas said.

Would Annie remain there if Harley or his associates had come to do them harm?

"Charlotte, are you in there?" Sheriff Wyatt McCallister called out.

"Yes. I'm here with Jonas Knowles," she replied. "The tunnel is collapsing. We're trapped."

"We're going to get you out of there," Wyatt assured her. "Hold on."

"Hurry," she urged. "There's a fire, and smoke is pouring in."

"We got you, Charlotte. You just stay close to the door where you can get some fresh air."

It was going to be okay. Despite everything Harley and his people had thrown at them, they were going to be okay.

The noise of what sounded like a tool being used to try and pry the door open could be heard over the noise of the fire.

"Wyatt, Harley Owens is behind this." Charlotte told the sheriff all they'd discovered. "He left the area in a side-by-side like the one out front."

The sheriff spoke to one of his people before answering. "We'll get him, Charlotte. The fire has just about burned what's left of the house. When we arrived, we were so afraid until we heard Annie barking."

Annie had saved their lives.

Jonas held Charlotte close as they kept near the door. The door eased open slightly, the fresh air rushing through the hole was pure bliss.

"We're almost there," the sheriff called out. "I've never seen a door like this one before. There's no door handle or lock. It's metal and several inches thick. I'm thinking Harley had some type of remote to close it, which would make it easy to close but without the property tools impossible to open."

Jonas was angry at the lengths Harley was willing to go to save himself and harm others.

Charlotte explained about Betty. "She has the four women who were taken with her."

A pause, then Wyatt said, "I'll send some men to get them and take them to the station. You probably saved their lives."

Charlotte told him about Sasha's role in things, as well. "He has her and she's in danger because she has things on Harley that will incriminate him."

Soon the last obstacle was removed from in front of the door, and it opened.

Jonas, still holding on to Charlotte, stepped from the nightmare of smoke and dust into the cold and snowy morning, and it had never felt more welcoming.

Blankets were placed over their shoulders. "Let's get you into my cruiser to warm up." The man whose voice Jonas recognized as the sheriff led them over to a Jeep bearing the sheriff's insignia on it.

He waited until both Jonas and Charlotte had slipped into the back seat before he got in and cranked the heater up high.

Sheriff Wyatt McCallister turned in his seat so he would see them.

"Sheriff, this is Jonas Knowles," Charlotte

said, gesturing to him. "I wouldn't be alive right now if it weren't for him."

"It's nice to meet you, Sheriff," Jonas said. "You and your people are a welcomed sight. Do you have any word on Abram and Lainey?"

The sheriff nodded. "She called earlier, and we picked her and Abram up. She was treated at the hospital. They are both safe at the station."

That was good news indeed.

"Both were too shaken up to make much sense," Sheriff McCallister continued, "but I have a suspicion whatever is happening here is huge."

Charlotte reached for Jonas's hand and explained to her boss what led her to Harley's house in the first place.

The sheriff's brow creased. "So, Harley kidnapped Lainey from near her work?"

"That's correct." Charlotte nodded. "Dottie called me in to help. I thought it would be just a simple matter of Lainey falling asleep in the camp." She shook her head. "Boy, was I wrong."

Charlotte remembered the ledger and the key she'd placed in her pocket. "There's something else you need to hear." She told him about Elliott Shores's involvement. "He's part of the ring, Wyatt. And there are others in high places involved."

"Like possibly the coroner," Jonas added.

The sheriff's frown deepened. "This is terrible."

"One more thing," Charlotte added. "Elliott and several others referred to the person in charge by the initials D.A." She looked to Jonas. "We haven't been able to figure out his name, though."

The sheriff scanned the tunnel area where his men were examining. "Do you have any idea how many men are in the woods looking for you?"

Jonas shook his head. "We lost track. There were several groups and I'm pretty sure we ran into some more than once. I'd say at least a dozen." Charlotte nodded in agreement.

"Stay put," the sheriff instructed. "I've called in extra manpower. Lainey and Abram told us about Elliott. I've alerted his chief to what he is being accused of. He had no idea one of his officers was involved in a human trafficking ring." Wyatt shook his head.

"I want to be part of the group who goes after Harley and the rest of the men," Charlotte told her superior.

He eyed her carefully. "You're exhausted. You need to go to the hospital and get checked out for smoke inhalation at the very least."

Charlotte shook her head, clearly ready to reject his suggestion. "I'm fine, Wyatt. This is too important. I want to see it through for Michaela and Ryan."

The sheriff's brows rose. "What are you talking about? Do you believe their deaths had something to do with this?"

"I do." Charlotte told him her suspicions.

McCallister leaned forward in his seat. "I never understood a lot of things about the case starting with Ryan's fall. He'd been through much more difficult situations than what he faced on the mountain that day."

"Exactly," Charlotte said. "I'm certain he spotted Michaela with whoever was trying to kill her and tried to help."

And whoever had Michaela had recognized Ryan, so he'd had to die, too. It sickened Jonas to imagine how many people's lives were sacrificed so they could keep doing what they were doing. How many others in authority were involved in this dreadful crime ring?

"I want to be part of bringing them down, too," Jonas told them both. For Charlotte but also for himself. He wanted to see Harley behind bars and make sure Betty would never have to deal with her abusive husband again. And all those men who had played a part in hurting so many innocents, he wanted them to be brought to justice and made to pay for what they'd done. They'd ruined so many lives because of greed.

"Not going to happen," McCallister said, facing him. "You're a civilian. I understand you're invested in this case, Jonas, but as these men have proven, they're dangerous and have everything to lose."

"Sheriff, come in." The police radio squawked to life.

The sheriff hit the mic attached to his jacket. "Go ahead, Rogers."

"We've spotted the side-by-side."

McCallister sat up straight. "Where?"

The deputy gave the coordinates.

"We're on our way." The sheriff gave the command to his team and put the Jeep into gear. "Buckle up. There's some rough terrain ahead."

Jonas snapped the seat belt into place and held on tight as the Jeep pulled out and barreled down the mountainside. Jonas prayed Harley would be taken alive. They needed answers that only he could provide.

SEVENTEEN

Wyatt slowed the vehicle to a crawl then stopped.

Charlotte noticed an officer heading their way. "That must be the one who spotted Harley."

The rest of the team pulled in behind Wyatt's vehicle.

"Sheriff," the deputy acknowledged once all three had exited the cruiser. "As far as I can tell, he's held up in a trapper's cabin a quarter of a mile down the mountain. I came across the side-by-side abandoned in the woods just up from here. It looks as if he ran out of fuel."

Wyatt's steely gaze scanned the area. "And how do you know he's still in the cabin?"

"I approached the cabin and saw movement inside. That's when I radioed you."

Wyatt nodded. "Since we don't have an idea of how many others may be in the cabin, we approach cautiously. Harley may be holding up with some people loyal to him." Wyatt directed several of his deputies to circle around behind the cabin. They would come from all directions.

"Jonas, you need to wait for us here," Charlotte told him. They'd gone through so much together. She couldn't bear it if something happened to him when they were so close to finishing this nightmare.

He reluctantly agreed.

She got out and followed Wyatt. As the team of law enforcement officers approached, Charlotte noticed that the cabin appeared to have only one window.

When they were still some distance away, Wyatt ordered them to halt. He radioed to the deputies around the back. "Any sign of Harley?"

"Negative, Sheriff. There's no window at the back, only a door. Should we keep going?"

"Affirmative."

Charlotte's hands shook on the weapon in her hand as the team edged toward the cabin.

"Take the door," Wyatt ordered the officers around back.

On Wyatt's command, the front entrance was breached. In a matter of seconds, they were inside, and the tense scene unfolded.

The cabin was larger than Jonas's. The team quickly cleared the living room and kitchen. One closed door remained.

Wyatt gestured toward the door. As they

neared, a barrage of shots flew through the wooden door, and everyone jumped back.

When silence returned, Wyatt moved to the door. He was a strong man who led by example. Wyatt kicked the door open. It slammed against the wall. Another round of shots had them backing away.

A click, click, click followed. "Go!" Charlotte yelled, and the team poured into the room. Harley held a knife against the throat of a noticeably emaciated woman with purple hair. Michaela had mentioned Sasha had purple hair... This was Sasha.

The young woman's frightened eyes latched on to Charlotte for help.

Wyatt stepped forward. "It's over, Harley. Let her go. There's no getting out of this. Drop the knife and get your hands in the air."

She'd never seen Harley look so freaked out before. "No way," he said while continually shaking his head. "You're going to kill me if I do."

"No one's going to hurt you," Wyatt assured him. "This is your chance to help yourself by bringing in the rest of those men. But you have to let her go."

Harley appeared to lose all color. "They'll kill me."

"We can protect you," Wyatt assured him.

Harley's hand on the knife shook. "You promise you aren't going to shoot me?"

"I'm the sheriff, Harley. I'm not going to let anyone hurt you. You have my word."

Harley's grip on Sasha tightened briefly before he let her go.

"Come to me," Charlotte told Sasha. The woman ran into Charlotte's open arms. "You're safe now." Sasha buried her face against Charlotte's shoulder.

But the situation wasn't over yet.

"Drop the knife, Harley," Wyatt said calmly. "We're almost finished but you need to drop the knife."

Harley stared at it as if he had forgotten he held it. He lowered his hand and placed the knife on the floor.

"Okay, now kick it over to me," Wyatt told him. Charlotte watched him do what he did best. Wyatt could make a victim, or a perp, feel as if they were his best friend.

Once the knife was out of Harley's reach, Wyatt picked it up and handed it to his deputy.

"Okay, I need you to put your hands behind your back, Harley. I'm going to cuff you and then we're taking you back to the station."

"You're going to kill me." Harley was practically in tears.

Wyatt kept eye contact with the man as he said,

"Now, Harley, I gave you my word. I'm not going to let anyone hurt you."

"All right, but I'm trusting you." Harley turned around and Wyatt cuffed him and led him from the room.

As he passed by them, Sasha shrank away.

"You're okay. Is your name Sasha?" Charlotte asked. She needed to be sure.

The young woman's surprise was clear. "Yes. How did you know?"

"Michaela told me."

Sasha flinched then tears filled her eyes. "I didn't mean for her to die. I was just trying to stay alive."

"It's okay," Charlotte said and led her to the living room where EMTs had arrived. "Let them check you out and then you will be transported to the sheriff's station for questioning. Is there someone we can call?"

Sasha's tears fell freely. "M-my parents. I haven't spoken to them in years."

While Sasha was treated, Charlotte stepped outside. Jonas left the vehicle and joined her.

She told him what happened. "I'm so glad Wyatt convinced him to surrender." She held up her shaking hands.

Jonas glanced around at the activity taking place. "I'm glad he's in custody but we still don't have any idea about the others."

"No, we don't." Charlotte looked toward the cruiser where Harley was being held. "Hopefully, he can help unravel the truth, along with Sasha. You're right about her. She's a victim."

Harley on the other hand, well, Charlotte wanted him to get what he deserved. Harley Owens should never see the outside of a prison again.

Wyatt found them. "This is something else," he said. "We have law enforcement agents scouring the woods for the rest of those involved." He glanced back at Harley. "My guess is, they'll hear the news soon enough and scatter."

"We can't let them get away, Wyatt. Every one of them needs to pay for what they've done." Charlotte couldn't imagine how someone sworn to protect the public could get involved in trafficking young women.

"I'm going to run Harley into town and get him processed. By the way, the other young women who were kidnapped are safe at the station and giving their statements." Wyatt blew out a sigh. "I'm guessing you want to be part of Harley's interview?"

"I do, but I want to be part of bringing in the rest of those men, as well, and I'm pretty sure we should start at the camp."

Wyatt nodded. "Let's bring those who hide in darkness to the light and make them show their faces."

* * *

The first set of vehicles parked some distance from the Christian camp. According to the team of law officers sitting on the camp, an unknown number of people were holed up inside.

Jonas had never had much dealing with law enforcement except for the occasional visits from Charlotte concerning Harley. Now, he found himself in a manhunt to bring down members of a trafficking ring and he understood the adrenaline rush that came from tracking down a bad guy.

"Are you doing okay?" Charlotte asked. She'd been keeping a close eye on him.

He swung her way. "Just ready to have this finished." Something shifted in her eyes, and she looked sad. Jonas wondered what he'd said to be responsible.

"It's almost over." She nodded. "Soon, you'll be able to return to your life."

Was it his imagination or was there a strain to her voice he hadn't heard before? Before he could ask her, several of her fellow law enforcement officers came over.

Charlotte turned away, and he doubted everything he'd once believed he thought she felt toward him. He'd opened his heart up again after losing Ivy—he'd thought for certain Charlotte returned his feelings—and yet the chilliness in her behavior now had him convinced he'd misread everything. "We have people in place around the camp. No one's getting through," Elliott's boss, Chief Harris, assured her.

Jonas didn't trust the chief fully. After all, Elliott was dirty. What if there were others? She nodded. "Let's hope they're all there."

"Do you trust him?" Jonas asked once the chief disappeared.

She turned to him and Jonas tried to recover from the impression he'd lost her,

"I do," she said quietly. "But I need you to stay here, Jonas." Charlotte drew her weapon and checked the magazine.

"All right." He reluctantly did as she asked but watched the band of law enforcement agents as they advanced toward the camp.

Clearing a place as big as the camp took time. They started with the living quarters and worked their way toward the center of the camp where the dining hall and the chapel were located.

Shots were fired near the dining hall. Jonas's fear for Charlotte's safety had him wanting to rush after her. He squinted through the sea of officers and spotted her. She was okay.

Several armed men appeared to be inside still and doing their best to hold off the police.

The officers exchanged shots with the criminals, peppering the walls of the dining hall until silence returned to the camp.

"Take the building," Chief Harris's command could be heard from where Jonas stood. Officers and deputies stormed it, and he knew Charlotte was among them.

He counted off every tense-filled minute until she and the rest of the officers exited the building. A half dozen cuffed men were led out.

Charlotte found him and came over.

"Was anyone hurt?" he asked.

She shook her head, her attention on the restrained men. "There's Elliott," she said in flat tone.

Shores kept his attention on the ground while his chief secured his hands behind his back.

Charlotte hurried over to the policeman. When Shores saw her, he looked as if he would have backed away if it weren't for Chief Harris holding on to him.

"You were my friend." Charlotte's hands clenched at her sides, her expression tight as she waited for Shores to speak but he didn't.

"You realized how important Ryan was to me, yet all this time you were part of the ones who killed him."

Shores flinched as if she'd struck him. "I don't know what you're talking about. I had nothing to do with Ryan's death."

His nervous denial proved his involvement in Jonas's mind.

"This is all a misunderstanding," Shores said. "I was working undercover to bring down this ring."

"That's not true!" He knew Charlotte wouldn't let him go on. "You're part of it. How could you? You have a wife and little girls." She turned away, a disgusted expression on her face.

"I *am* working undercover," the cop insisted. "I found out about what was happening and decided to go undercover."

Charlotte whirled back to him. "If that's so then why doesn't your chief here have knowledge about your doings?" Shores didn't have an answer.

Jonas watched alongside Charlotte as the guilty were led away.

"We still don't have the one in charge," she said in frustration. "And I have a feeling these men will be too afraid to speak his name."

Jonas couldn't get the key out of his head. "I realize we searched Harley's house before, but we never found a safe. He could have hidden it."

"You're right." Charlotte motioned to one of the deputies. "Brad, can I use your cruiser?" She told him where they were headed.

"Sure." He tossed her the keys. "I can catch a ride. I have a suspicion we're going to be busy booking all these men for a while. Do you need backup?"

The stakes were high. Finding the evidence as quick as possible was imperative. Charlotte looked at Jonas before shaking her head. "We've got this. Do you mind if I take your phone?" she asked Brad. "Mine was destroyed. I'll let Wyatt know where we're going."

"Okay." Brad handed her his phone. "Be careful. Call if you need help."

Charlotte loaded Annie into the back seat of the police car while Jonas got into the passenger side. She fired the engine and slowly eased from the camp while Jonas recalled the terrifying moments they'd gone through here.

"I'm glad Abram and Lainey are safe, as well as those women," he said. "But there were others who weren't so lucky. If we can save them still…"

"I hope so. Hang on," Charlotte warned as the path in front of them grew rough.

Jonas grabbed the dash as the cruiser rocked over some downed trees.

"Sorry about that." She glanced his way.

More than anything, Jonas wanted to open his heart up and tell her what he felt for her and yet…

If he were to admit his feelings—if he let himself become that vulnerable again and she rejected him, Jonas wasn't sure he'd recover from a blow like that.

EIGHTEEN

Charlotte could almost sense the tension in Jonas. He kept looking her way. He wanted to ask her about the way she'd reacted to him earlier. But how could she answer him when she wasn't sure herself. Why had she hesitated? Every time she looked at Jonas, she thought about Ryan and the unfinished business standing in their way.

She eased the cruiser onto the road that ran past Jonas's house.

"Do you believe we have all the men?" he asked with a hint of uneasiness in his tone.

She blew out a sigh, just happy they were talking again. "I sure hope so. Except for the person who's in charge, but then I doubt he gets his hands dirty, and if he's gotten wind of what's been happening, he could have fled the county by now."

Charlotte prayed that she was wrong about the coroner being involved. It was bad enough Elliott had betrayed his oath.

"I feel sorry for Betty." Jonas sighed. "She doesn't work. How's she going to survive this?"

Charlotte touched his arm. "We'll do what we can to help her. She doesn't deserve to lose everything because of her husband's crimes."

As they reached the spot where she'd begun her search for Lainey, Charlotte shivered when she thought about how close to death she'd come. Did Elliott have any knowledge she'd been taken, and that Harley was planning to kill her? The betrayal she felt at the thought of Elliott okaying her murder shook her to her core.

She made the bend in the road, and the house sat as another reminder of what had happened.

Charlotte rolled the cruiser to a stop. The darkness of the house gave her the creeps.

"Here, take this…just in case." Charlotte handed him the extra weapon she'd taken from one of Harley's people. She unholstered her weapon and opened the door. Jonas did the same. She carefully closed the door and panned the area looking for anything that might spell trouble. Nothing but silence. She opened the back door and let Annie out. The dog sniffed the ground and headed around the corner of the house like before.

Jonas shot her a look. "Is she on something?"

"I'm not sure." With her weapon drawn and ready, Charlotte eased around the corner of the house with Jonas at her six.

The dog had reached the back porch and was sniffing around. When she spotted Charlotte, Annie wagged her tail and Charlotte relaxed. "She's just following scents—nothing in particular." The relief she felt at not having to face down another bad guy made her knees feel weak.

At the back door, Charlotte glanced through the kitchen and what was visible of the living room. "I don't see anyone." She slowly opened the door and stepped inside.

When they'd come here earlier, she and Jonas were looking for the missing women. They'd searched the place but hadn't been looking for a safe.

"We stay together," Charlotte instructed. Starting in the kitchen, Charlotte began opening cabinets. "Don't overlook anything. It's possible Harley could have a small lockbox the size of a shoebox or maybe something bigger." And it was possible the key fit a safe-deposit box of something they might never find. She struggled not to give in to the doubts.

Jonas took the opposite side of the kitchen, and they searched through every cabinet and drawer.

"Nothing here." Charlotte placed her hands on her hips. "The laundry room." They'd given it only a cursory look before.

She hurried through the opening off the kitchen, which led to the room containing a washer and dryer, a small sink and several cabinets. "Please be here." Yet after searching the final cabinet, they were no closer to finding the safe than before.

"What about in one of the closets?" Jonas suggested.

"It's possible." There was still lots of house to check. Yet her sinking sensation wouldn't let her go.

In the hall, there were closets on either side. While Jonas checked one, Charlotte opened the door to the other. It was crammed full of junk. She blew out a frustrated sigh and started digging.

"Anything?" Jonas asked once he'd finished his search.

"Not yet."

He came over and knelt beside her. While he worked, she glanced at his strong profile. Exhaustion clung to him as it did her, yet he'd never once faltered in backing her up. He was a strong and handsome man, and she cared deeply for him. She might even... She couldn't let herself say the word *love*. She'd loved Ryan but hadn't thought herself capable of giving her heart to someone else.

Jonas glanced her way. She turned her attention to a box she'd dragged out to look through.

After an exhausting search, the closet yielded nothing useful. "Let's try the living room."

Yet with each room cleared, the hope of finding evidence to identify the person in charge dwindled.

"I wonder if Harley will cooperate to save himself," Jonas suggested after he'd seen her disappointment.

She smiled. "I hope so. I doubt that he has any loyalty to the person who tried to kill him."

"No, Harley's always struck me as the type of person who's only after what is best for him."

Once the final room was searched, the truth became clear. "It's not here," Charlotte managed to get out. "I sure hope we can get Harley to tell us what the key fits." She started for the front of the house when a sound at the back, where Annie had been, grabbed her attention. "Did you hear that?"

Jonas frowned as he started back through the house. "I did."

They reached the back door and Charlotte looked out. Annie was no longer there. "She may have spotted an animal in the woods and gave chase." Before she stepped from the house, she glanced toward the laundry room once more. Something caught her eye. The thickness of the wall was different on the left.

She stopped and pointed it out to Jonas. "There's something off there."

"You're right," he agreed. "Almost as if something has been built into the wall."

She faced him. "We have to break it down."

Charlotte moved to the wall and tapped around. "It appears hollow." She tried the butt of her weapon to smash the Sheetrock. While it worked, it would take forever to get it free. "Did you see any tools in the house?"

Jonas's face brightened. "Yes, in the hall. I'll be right back." When he returned, he had a couple of hammers with him. "These should work."

Charlotte laid her weapon on the washer opposite them and started swinging the claw part of the hammer. She and Jonas worked together and soon they had a great deal of the wall removed. She flashed her light into the space. "I see something. Hang on." She reached down and grabbed hold of a metal box and pulled it out. "Let's take it to the kitchen where the light is better."

Her hands shook as she carried the box into the kitchen and brought out the key.

With Jonas standing close, she slipped the key into the box, and it opened. She flipped the lid up.

Another ledger was inside much like the one she'd found at the mountain cabin. But this one had names of the people involved in the trafficking ring.

She stood back, amazed at the list of people involved in this.

"Do you see D.A.'s real name?" Jonas asked, looking over her shoulder.

Charlotte began flipping through the pages when a noise nearby grabbed her attention. She looked up and the ledger fell from her hand in shock.

"Phillip?" Phillip Hollins, the county's district attorney, stood in the entrance of the kitchen with a weapon drawn on them. Suddenly everything fell into place. D.A. They'd been looking at the two letters as initials, but it wasn't the leader's initials but his job title.

A sad smile spread across Phillip's face. "You found it. I've been searching all over for that ledger. Kick it over to me."

"Wait, I've seen you before," Jonas whispered. Charlotte saw the shock on his face. "You're the one who pretended to be Betty's nephew."

The betrayal cut like a knife.

"Now, Charlotte." Phillip's kindly tone from before turned hard and unrecognizable.

She and Phillip had worked on many cases together. She'd testified for him lots of times. He and Ryan were best friends and had been since grade school.

She kicked the ledger over. He slowly squatted until he could pick it up while keeping his eyes and the weapon on them.

"How could you? Ryan was your best friend."

Phillip had given the eulogy at Ryan's funeral and all the while he was the one responsible for his death.

Something flittered across his face. Regret perhaps. "Yes, well, it was the hardest thing I've ever had to do. I wish it hadn't had to be that way, but Ryan saw me with the girl. He figured out I was involved. I didn't have a choice."

"You had a choice. You could have turned yourself in, but you chose your life over Ryan's and Michaela's."

He looked at her as if she were talking nonsense. "I couldn't go to prison with people I'd put behind bars. They'd kill me." Phillip stuffed the ledger into his jacket. "Harley—he was such an amateur. I should never have gotten him involved. I figured he'd eventually get us all in trouble."

She had placed Brad's phone in her right pocket. Charlotte stepped a little behind Jonas and brought the phone out enough to press the 9-1-1 keys. She prayed the dispatcher could hear enough of the conversation to realize what was happening and send help.

"We thought D.A. was the initials of a person, but it wasn't. It's your position. Phillip Hollins, district attorney," she said loudly.

Phillip looked at her strangely. "We've been over this already."

Beside her, Charlotte noticed Jonas slip his

hand in his pocket where his weapon was. It was their only chance.

Charlotte stepped forward enough to hide the activity from Phillip.

"How long have you been involved in trafficking young women, Phillip? How long have you assisted Harley and who knows how many others in getting off when they were guilty?"

Phillip's face contorted in anger. "I didn't have a choice. Harley told me if I didn't help him stay out of jail, he'd go to the police and tell them everything. He said he had a ledger with everyone's names in it that he'd hidden away someplace safe where it wouldn't be found."

She had to keep him talking. "Why did you go after Michaela?"

Phillip's mouth twisted. "I was there at the party the night Sasha brought Michaela there. She saw me... Michaela knew who I was. I'm not sure why she didn't mention seeing me at the party. And I couldn't take the chance she'd keep her mouth shut." He grimaced. "Sasha screwed up by picking Michaela as one of our girls," he spat. "I couldn't risk Michaela changing her mind and going to the police with my name. So, I followed her for a while. She confronted me— told me she was going to tell the police I was involved. I couldn't let that happen."

"So, you kidnapped her," Charlotte said, trying to draw the conversation out while her heart was breaking at what he said.

"Yes. I brought her up to the mountain. I had it all planned out. I'd make it look like a suicide. Michaela was distraught over her missing friend, Sasha. Only Ryan showed up and tried to save her. We fought and I— He fell off the mountain. It was an accident."

Charlotte's stomach clenched. It was a lie. She struggled to keep the pain in when she thought about Ryan's reaction to realizing his friend wanted to kill him.

"So, you killed Ryan and then made Michaela's death look like a suicide, and you got your buddy at the coroner's office to fudge the truth."

Phillip didn't hesitate to confess to everything, likely because he planned to kill them. But then he stopped talking suddenly. "Hey, what are you up to? You've called someone."

He lunged for Charlotte. Jonas pushed her behind him and whipped out his weapon. Down the road, sirens blared. Phillip fired several shots off before Jonas could get a single one off.

Jonas fell to the ground. He'd been shot.

"Jonas!" Charlotte screamed and grabbed the weapon he'd dropped. She fired once. The shot struck Phillip's chest. He hit the floor. Charlotte quickly removed his weapon and felt for a pulse.

He was still alive. But right now, all she could think about was she might be losing Jonas.

She dropped down beside Jonas. He stared up at her with fear on his face.

Charlotte unbuttoned his jacket. Blood covered his shirt near his stomach and was quickly spreading. "It's going to be okay," she whispered and grabbed a towel from the counter and placed it against the wound. "Hold on. Help is coming." She grabbed her phone from her pocket. "Dispatch, are you there?"

"I'm here, Charlotte," Ruby answered immediately. "Help should be there soon."

"I need medical attention, as well. Two gunshot victims."

"They're arriving, as well. Hold on."

Charlotte dropped the phone beside her and kept pressure on Jonas's wound. Soon the sirens stopped out front and the house was breached by law enforcement, including Wyatt.

Wyatt ordered men to action. "We need EMTs in here now!"

Two medics ran into the kitchen. One knelt beside Phillip.

"I've got him," Vince, the lead paramedic, assured her as he gently pushed Charlotte out of the way and he and his partner went to work on Jonas.

Jonas's eyes closed as he lost consciousness.

"No." Charlotte covered her mouth with her hand as tears filled her eyes. She couldn't lose him.

The medics worked quickly to get Jonas ready to transport.

"I'm going with him," Charlotte told the two EMTs as the gurney was raised and they headed for the front of the house.

"Go, we've got this," Wyatt called after her.

A second ambulance arrived and two more EMTs took over working on Phillip.

Jonas's gurney was loaded into the ambulance and Charlotte climbed in along with Vince. With lights strobing, they rushed along to Elk Ridge Memorial.

Jonas looked so pale, and he still hadn't regained consciousness.

"He's lost a lot of blood," Vince told her. He hung an IV and packed and bandaged the wound.

They raced down the road and whipped out onto the county road leading to town.

Once they reached the city limits, Dennis, the driver, turned onto the exit for the hospital. As soon as they reached the hospital doors, Vince hopped out and Charlotte followed. Soon, a wealth of medical personnel greeted them, and Jonas was escorted to the ER for examination while Vince ran down his vitals and explained what happened to the attending.

"The bullet is lodged inside. It appears to have nicked his spleen," Vince told the doctor.

Within minutes of the confirmation, Jonas was on his way up to surgery. Charlotte rushed along beside the team. She didn't want to leave his side.

Once they reached the operating room floor, the nurse stopped her. "I'm sorry, deputy, but you'll have to wait here."

Charlotte stopped and watched as Jonas was pushed through the swinging door.

The nurse smiled. "I promise I'll let you know the minute we have word."

It would have to do. "Thank you."

The nurse disappeared behind the doors and Charlotte paced around the waiting area, too worried to sit.

She was making her dozenth or more lap around the circle she'd created when someone stepped from the elevator. It was Wyatt.

She hurried toward him. "Is there word on Phillip?"

"We had to remove his spleen, but he'll be okay."

Charlotte bent over relieved. "Oh, thank goodness. We need him to cooperate." She hugged Wyatt. "Thank you."

He patted her shoulder. "We still have a long way to go to uncover all the players, but thanks to the names in the ledger, it won't take long.

You were right about the coroner. He's one of the names listed there. My men are on their way to arrest him now."

She tried to take it all in. "That's unbelievable. And Elliott? He tried to claim he was working undercover."

"Yeah, well, his name is in the ledger, too, and I have a suspicion he's going to back off of the claim soon enough."

She remembered where she'd hidden Harley's phone and told him about it. "How many girls have they taken through the years?" Charlotte couldn't take in the amount of destruction these people had caused.

"We aren't sure, but I have a feeling the first ledger you recovered will tell us. And Harley is screaming he wants to talk. He'll be able to fill in some blanks."

"As long as he doesn't get a lower sentence because of it."

Wyatt assured her he wouldn't. "What's Jonas's prognosis?"

Charlotte swallowed deeply. "He lost a lot of blood, and the bullet nicked his spleen. They're going to have to remove it. Hopefully, there won't be any additional internal damage." Getting those words out was hard.

"He's in good hands." Wyatt looked her in the eye. "Something happening between you two?"

Charlotte wasn't ready to talk about it. The realization she'd fallen in love with Jonas was still too new.

"Never mind." Wyatt held up his hands. "It won't be like Ryan, Charlotte. I have a feeling Jonas is going to be okay." With another pat on the arm, Wyatt left her to the self-realization that, despite her attempts to deny it and cling to the past and her guilt over Ryan, that part of her life was over. Ryan had loved her, but she couldn't bring him back.

She turned toward the double doors. Her future was in there, fighting for his life.

Please God, don't let him die.

When the exhaustion of running for their lives caught up with her, Charlotte found a chair close by so she could watch those double doors. And she sat and kept her focus on them and the future waiting for her.

After several hours, the same nurse who'd stopped her earlier came out and Charlotte leaped to her feet.

"How is he?" Charlotte frantically searched the woman's face. When it broke into a smile, everything in her body relaxed.

"He's going to be okay. He made it through the surgery. They removed his spleen but there's no other signs of damage. As soon as he's moved to a room, I'll come get you and you can see him."

Charlotte clutched her arm. "Thank you."

Every inch of her body rejoiced in the knowledge she had the chance to tell Jonas how happy she was to have met him and how much she prayed he felt the same way.

Jonas opened his eyes. The world around him was fuzzy. He blinked until shapes became objects and he realized he was in a hospital. The last moments before he collapsed flashed through his head. That man was going to shoot Charlotte. He'd pushed her away but hadn't been able to stop what happened. The pain had dropped him to the floor. He remembered her leaning over him telling him he was going to be okay.

"You're awake."

Jonas turned toward her voice. Charlotte was seated beside him holding his hand.

"Hey," he managed in a voice that was below a whisper. It didn't matter because her smile was all he needed.

"Hey yourself." Her smile was the best thing he'd seen in a while.

She told him Phillip had been arrested. Then someone knocked on the door and Jonas's attention reluctantly left her.

Sheriff McCallister stood in the doorway. "I heard you were awake." He came inside and stopped beside Charlotte. "It's good to hear you're going to be okay. When you're feeling better, I'm going to need both your statements."

Jonas nodded. "How are the women? Betty?" He felt responsible for his neighbor and the victims.

"Fine," Wyatt said. "I'm certain Betty's relieved her time with Harley is over. He had her terrified to do anything on her own." Wyatt shook his head. "She told me he forced her to break off all family relationships. Did you know she has a sister who lives in Idaho?"

Jonas was surprised by that. "No. I assumed her family was all gone."

The sheriff shrugged. "She called her sister and she's going to stay with her for a while."

Jonas was relieved. "I'm glad to hear it."

Wyatt's expression turned grim. "Harley is talking. He implicated Phillip in both Ryan's and Michaela's deaths, but then you both knew as much since Phillip pretty much confessed to the murders in front of you. With the ledger, we have the names of the people involved and the arrests are happening right now. Locating the women won't be as easy. They're spread out across the country—probably others are in different countries. Harley was able to give us the names of the contacts in those other locations, and we're reaching out to law enforcement in those cities." He shrugged again. "I'm hopeful."

Despite what they'd gone through to identify the victims, those young women who were forced into a life of prostitution were changed forever.

"Well, I'm heading back to the station. I'll stop by in a few days and get both your statements." He nodded to Jonas and clamped Charlotte's shoulder briefly before leaving.

Jonas couldn't take his eyes off Charlotte. Now that she had the truth, he couldn't imagine the thoughts going through her head. "How are you doing with all this?"

She reached for his hand once more. "I'm at peace," she said, surprising him. "I always wondered if Ryan's death was really an accident or if Michaela didn't kill herself. Now her parents can have the truth about what happened. I hope the truth will give them some measure of closure." She stopped as if to gather her thoughts. "It breaks my heart to think Ryan had to die at the hands of someone he trusted, yet both Phillip and Harley will pay for their crimes. I guess that's some small comfort."

He thought about losing Ivy. Charlotte had someone tangible to blame for Ryan's death. But for Jonas there was only him.

She clutched his hand tighter, and he focused on her face. "For the first time since Ryan's death, I have hope for the future." She was smiling and he couldn't look away. It was as if the weight of the world had been lifted from her.

"Why do you have hope?" he asked without looking away and prayed he would be part of it.

"Because of you," she said softly. "I'm so grateful God brought you into my life, Jonas." She leaned closer. "We both have a chance at happiness…together." She waited for him to speak, but he was incapable because she'd just told him she wanted to be with him. And no words could have brought more joy. "I finally realized guilt has no place in the future. I love you, Jonas. But if you stand a chance at moving beyond Ivy's death, you must find a way to forgive yourself. Neither of us can rewrite the past, but together, we can have a future filled with happiness again. We can step out of the shadows of the past and walk in the light." She looked so vulnerable as she waited for him to answer.

Tears filled his eyes. He wanted to hold on to her hand and step into that future with her. "I love you, too. And I'll do everything in my power to make our lives together happy."

And he would. Ivy was his past. Charlotte— this beautiful woman had helped him see the past couldn't be changed. He was ready to let go of his guilt once and for all and embrace Charlotte's love because the future, well, it was wide-open.

EPILOGUE

Eighteen months later...

"Are you sure you want to put the house up for sale?" Charlotte asked him once more as they finished packing the last of his things into her SUV.

He knew she worried about him wanting to return to the Amish ways, but that wasn't who he was anymore. And he was finally happy with his life.

Jonas smiled at the woman who was now his wife. He reached for her hand and touched the simple gold wedding band she wore.

They'd married in a small ceremony at the church he'd started attending with her. Abram was there as his best man. Jonas had invited Ivy's parents and he'd been thrilled when they'd come. They were making small steps at repairing their relationship.

Lainey had stood up for Charlotte. Most of those who attended were law enforcement. In the months since the ordeal with Harley, Jonas had become friends with them all.

"I'm sure." He leaned over and kissed her tenderly. He loved her so much. She was the blessing from *Gott* he never expected to receive.

A few weeks back, Jonas had reached out to a realtor in the area and discussed putting his house up for sale. He'd long since moved the cattle and his mare, Sandy, to Charlotte's ranch. Jonas was glad Sandy had returned to his place the day after she'd run away from the river.

"It's time." He wrapped his arm around her waist. Since Harley's arrest and upcoming trial, Betty had the house they'd shared together leveled. The property had sold recently. Jonas was happy to see Betty moving on. She'd stopped by with her sister, and she looked like a different person.

He and Charlotte had learned that the place Harley claimed was his in the mountains actually belonged to Phillip. They'd used it to transport the women through the mountains and into a waiting vehicle that would take them to the next stop along the line of the trafficking chain. But Harley had gotten greedy and begun trafficking stolen electronics along with weapons without his partners knowing. Harley's deceit and incompetence was the reason he'd been targeted for death.

Jonas and Charlotte stepped from his old house

and into the sunlit day. At times, it was hard to imagine the terrible things they'd gone through in these woods.

Since their escape, Lainey and Abram had formed a close relationship that had become a burgeoning romance. Lainey had confided in Charlotte that she wanted to become Amish so she and Abram could wed. During one of her visits to the ranch, Dottie told them she could see the change in her granddaughter, and she was happy Lainey had found someone to love.

While Jonas was fully embracing the life of an *Englischer*, he'd told Charlotte he wanted to track down the owners of the Christian camp and buy it with the proceeds from the sale of his place. He wanted something good to replace all the ugly things that had taken place there.

His plan was to open a camp for troubled teens to come for healing. Perhaps even for some of the women who had been abused by Harley and his crew. If he could use his skills as a former Amish man to teach young people how to do things with their hands, he'd be pleased. Abram had volunteered to assist, and Charlotte was all on board, as well.

"I still can't fathom it's been over a year," Charlotte murmured and turned to face him. "So many wonderful things have happened. I barely remember the bad anymore."

He brushed back a strand of hair from her face. Something was on her mind and his heart clenched. "Is everything okay?" Charlotte's troubled face reminded him of all that he stood to love, like he had with Ivy.

A smile spread across her face. "Yes, everything is fine. More than fine. I've been trying to find a way to tell you something for a while."

He froze, and she quickly assured him it was good news.

"I'm pregnant, Jonas. We're going to have a baby." She studied him closely. "How does that make you feel?"

He'd made so many mistakes with Ivy during her pregnancy. Jonas had vowed if *Gott* gave him another chance at being a father, he would be there beside Charlotte every step of the way.

"Happy," he managed while tears filled his eyes. "I'm so happy. You make me so happy." He drew her into his arms and held her close. This woman who had changed his life for the better. "I love you, Charlotte. So much."

She pulled away and smiled up at him. "I love you, too. And I'm so happy." She went back into his arms, and he stared into the distance at the Root Mountains, arrayed in their early fall shades of golds and oranges. The crispness in the air held a hint of the winter to come. For the first time in so long he looked forward to what each day brought. He was no longer existing day to day, going through the motions of what had to be done. He was living. Really living.

"Let's go home." He kissed her forehead.

Charlotte held his hand as they covered the distance to the SUV where Annie waited for them.

Jonas held the door open for Charlotte, then got in and petted the dog who was like family to him—she went everywhere with them.

"When?" he asked, and she looked over at him. He'd been content to let her drive although he had recently gotten his license.

"In six months." She smiled. "My next appointment is soon."

"I want to be there." He wanted to be part of everything.

She smiled and squeezed his hand as if she hadn't thought differently.

Jonas sat back in his seat and watched her maneuver the SUV away from the house that didn't hold any good memories. She turned toward the ranch, which had been in her family for years, and toward their future. They'd made many good memories there already. And, with the arrival of their child, he couldn't wait for what would come next.

* * * * *

Dear Reader,

In an instant, life can change. When solid ground disappears beneath our feet, we can lose hold of the things that seem important. Yet no matter how bad our circumstances get, if we trust God, He will see us through it all. Sometimes, it takes shaking ourselves free of what we think is best for Him to take us down the path He knows is right for us.

That's what happened to Charlotte and Jonas in *Deadly Mountain Escape*. Both suffered great losses in their lives. The pain of those wounds have left them frozen in the past.

Then, an unexpected call sends Deputy Charlotte Walker on a rush to find a missing friend where she ends up almost dying at the hands of a human trafficker.

But thanks to Jonas Knowles, who had a bad feeling about his neighbor, she and her friend Lainey are saved. With the help of Jonas, Charlotte and her K-9 partner Annie embark on a frantic race to save young women from a human trafficking ring operating in the county. In the process, they unravel the secrets of a year-long mystery and end up finding love again with each other.

Like Charlotte and Jonas, sometimes our

plans shatter around our feet, but with God's help, everything turns out according to His perfect design.

Many, many blessings,
Mary Alford